He pulled out a Smith and
Wesson 9mm from the back of
his pants, pointing it at the
side of her head.

She saw the gun just for a
second, then closed her eyes
tight. She knew what was
coming next.

A bullet to her temple.

DANGEROUS PASSION

by

Elly Stevens

❧ *1* ❧

Lauren sat across the table from her lover—and his wife. Well, he wasn't really her lover, yet. They hadn't made love, yet. They hadn't even gotten to know each other, yet. But they had kissed.

It was an accident. She was coming out of the break room; he was going in. As they collided, he had his hands up as if to brace himself, which conveniently landed on her breasts. They were both aghast, and slowly backed away from each other. He was apologetic, but with a hint of a smile. She was also apologetic, but she didn't mean it. It was the biggest thrill of her work day.

She had seen him before. Sometimes they said hi; sometimes they didn't. But on the following Friday night after "the incident," she saw him with friends at the bar of a nearby restaurant, George's Bar & Grill, which was packed with patrons who were thirsty after a long work week. They spied each other, but she resisted the urge to walk right up to him. After all, she knew nothing about him. He could be married. And he was.

During the next two hours, and after two lemon drop martinis, Lauren lost her inhibitions and smiled at him. He smiled back and walked over with his glass of whiskey and ginger. He introduced himself as Jack Kenner, a marketing rep for Beeler Printing.

"Oh," she thought. *"One of those."* Reps had a reputation for having a girl in every town they called in. She was a bit disappointed, but he was very attractive—about five foot, ten inches tall, thick, dark brown hair with a few gray streaks, blue eyes, no facial hair, toned build, and a kind smile. He wore a gray suit with a blue tie (that matched the color of his eyes), and a starched long-sleeved white shirt with cufflinks.

"Hi, I'm Lauren Miller. I work at Beeler, too, but in Supply Chain. It's nice to meet you, Jack."

He noted that she was a bit flirty and friendly, yet mature and confident. He liked that. She stood about five foot, eight inches tall, and was dressed professionally in a white summer linen suit with navy trim and wore navy pumps. Her wavy brown hair kept falling over her left eye and she kept pushing it out of the way. It came right back, only to be pushed away again. He noticed that she wasn't wearing a ring.

"Have you worked there long?" he inquired.

"For ten years. I'm usually tied to my computer. I imagine you're on the road a lot."

"Quite a bit. When there aren't equipment issues, I do cold calls. It keeps me busy."

Their conversation was badly timed, however, as her Uber showed up. She briefly looked over her shoulder at the door. "Oh, I have to go. Maybe I'll see you around the office," Lauren hinted with a smile. She gave him a goodbye hug. Before she could pull away, he briefly kissed her on the lips. Electricity shot through her body and her brown eyes looked directly into his liquid blue eyes, where she detected more than just a "goodbye." She wished that she knew more about him and she wanted another kiss, but she had to leave. She smiled at him once again, then pulled away. He watched her as she went out to the waiting car and glanced back his way. Putting her left foot into the car first before sitting, she gave him a chance to admire her right leg at the curb. He took it all in.

After his "move," Jack wondered if he did the right thing with his impulsive decision to kiss her. He was sure some of his co-workers had seen it, but most were a little tipsy and didn't think anything of it. It was just a kiss goodbye. Secretly, he hoped that the kiss might ensure another encounter. It might also kill the next opportunity if she was offended. He felt he had to chance it. Snooze, you lose.

Neither one of them was a "spring chicken." Jack was 42 and Lauren was 38. She had been married once for "five minutes" when she discovered that her husband was not the same person he was when they dated. Once married, he became a control freak who had to know her every move. In fact, he was known to follow her around. He even used a cell phone app to locate her without her knowledge, so he knew where she was at all times. It should have been a "red flag," but she never saw it coming. He was also heavily involved in gambling, which destroyed their savings quickly.

It was difficult for Lauren to date after the divorce. It seemed that all the "mature" (in age) men were either married, divorced with children, divorced with emotional baggage, momma's boys, sports fanatics who hung out with their "bros," heavy boozers, or drug users. She wanted a hard-working man who was financially and emotionally secure. Someone who would recognize her abilities and accomplishments. Someone who was crazy in love with her. Someone who was as passionate about her as she was about him. So, Lauren had spent the last decade of her life in celibacy. Not that she wanted to be celibate, but time went by and there were no men in her life. She spent many lonely nights wishing she had someone by her side. But it seemed that her ideal man was just a dream. Plus, her job kept her very busy—too busy to think about men or sex.

Jack made her think about sex, however—and her lack of sex over the years. She could still feel his soft lips on hers and she replayed the kiss in her mind over and over all the way home and during the night. She felt elated, anxious, sad, and lonely, all at the same time. She certainly wasn't feeling like herself. Jack occupied her thoughts that night and, in fact, she couldn't get him out of her mind the entire weekend. He wasn't on any social media sites, so she couldn't check him out.

On Saturday, Lauren looked at herself in a full-length mirror. She really hadn't taken care of herself over the years as well as she could have. "Why bother?" had been her motto. But now, things were different. She wanted to look her best—to be appealing, at least. She never thought she would be one of those women who went gaga over some man. It was shameful. She was an intelligent, decisive, career-driven woman who didn't need a man in her life. But was she lying to herself? Why was she suddenly so weak? So concerned about her appearance? So willing and ready to change—for a man?

If Jack thought she was confident, he was wrong. Perhaps in her job, but not in her personal life. She seemed to make all the wrong choices in her past. Was this the right choice? Or was this another bad decision. *"Time will tell,"* she thought.

What if Jack were married? How would she feel about that? Lauren decided, right then and there, that she would have to let her feelings go. That's all there was to it.

Lauren rummaged through her closet to find her best work clothes for Monday, when she hoped to run into Jack. She was dismayed that most of her wardrobe was ancient. She ripped blouses, skirts, slacks, and jackets off the hangers and threw them into a heap, along with some shabby sweaters. Then she stuffed them into a plastic bag and drove to the nearest Salvation Army collection site to drop them off.

"There! Now I have to buy new clothes!" she said aloud with satisfaction, as she sat in her silver Honda Civic sedan.

Her next stop was the mall. She was on a mission. How many times had she intended to buy some trendy items and then didn't? Way too many times. She started with undergarments, splurging on bras, panties, and a green silk nightgown with spaghetti straps. Then she tried on and bought several different outfits appropriate for work, and one little black dress for special occasions. It cost her a fortune, but she could afford it. She also had a manicure and pedicure, and stopped at the cosmetic store for a fresh, new supply of makeup. She felt like a new woman. A determined woman. A woman with a goal: another kiss from handsome Jack Kenner. And then...? She wanted to daydream about that. Perhaps her dreams would come true.

Now, if only she could make it through the day on Monday without losing concentration on her work as a supply chain assistant manager at Beeler Printing Products in Delaware where she improved productivity, quality, and process efficiency. Instead, Lauren found herself worrying needlessly about silly things like: What if Jack is on the road for a month? What if Jack doesn't remember who I am? What if Jack is a "player?" Was she really that desperate? She didn't know. She didn't remember ever feeling like this before. He had taken over her mind. She was obsessed.

She also had to prove to herself that she was still very much a woman. She needed to feel loved and wanted. She wanted to reciprocate that with passionate lovemaking—at some point. She hoped she could still do "it." That was a scary thought—what if she couldn't? What if she didn't feel the passion as she expected? Would it come later? How much would her nerves play into it? Could she get beyond her nerves and just relax? Maybe he was just what she needed.

Monday arrived at a snail's pace. Usually, weekends flew by, but not this weekend. This time she was looking forward to work. This time she wasn't thinking about her agenda. This time she had someone to seek out. She didn't dare ask around the office about Jack. It wouldn't be professional and there was no sense in letting the cat out of the bag.

She didn't want to be obvious about her interest, especially if he were married, so she kept everything to herself.

Just that thought alone made her unsure about her own intentions. Was she desperate enough to chase after a married man? She didn't want to believe that she might. But she might. It all depended on the circumstances.

There was no sure-fire way to know if Jack had just been a tease by kissing her. Perhaps he was even laughing at her! Now that would piss her off! However, there was no point in thinking negative thoughts, she decided. *"Think positive!"* was her new motto.

Toward the end of the workday, she finally caught a glimpse of Jack. So, he was in the office after all! He was looking at the bulletin board, where there were sheets of items for sale, cats and dogs available to good homes, and various services for computers, handyman work, et cetera.

"See anything you want?" she asked coyly, as she walked up next to him.

He turned, and with a grin, said, "I do now!" Feeling that same electricity go through her body, she blushed and smiled back.

She noted that he was looking at the announcement of a retirement party for one of the managers. "Are you going?" she inquired. Lauren then noticed that he wasn't wearing a ring and she let out a sigh of relief.

"Yeah, I think it would be a good idea to show my face. You can never network too much. How about you?"

"I think I will," Lauren said with her mind made up. She hoped that she could get to know him better and that it would be the first step in their relationship.

"See you there!" He winked and left her standing there with a feeling of excitement. Her heart was racing; her feet weren't touching the ground, or at least that's the way it seemed.

"Oh, my God; oh, my God; oh, my God," she kept repeating in a whisper while shaking her hands on the way back to her desk. She hadn't been this excited in years.

She had to make it through another work week before she saw Jack again. Finally, the night of the retirement party arrived. It was there, at the country club in their town, where she saw his face in a crowd. Lauren was wearing her new little black dress with a colorful infinity scarf around her neck, and tall high heels. Her hair was swept back to reveal her long, white neck and dangling gold earrings. She felt confident and beautiful. She walked over to him and greeted him with a smile.

"Jack, nice to see you." (What she meant was, "Jack, I want to make passionate love to you.")

"Lauren, nice to see you, too! I want you to meet my wife, Italia. Italia, this is Lauren."

It was like a bullet to her heart. She wondered if her facial expression showed her shock and disappointment. She gritted her teeth and smiled at Italia. She wanted to run away. She wanted to cry. She thought, *"No, no! Damn! This can't be happening!"* But it was. She had to accept it.

Italia was youthful, tall, slim yet very shapely, with beautiful dark eyes and generous red lips. Her jet-black hair glimmered under the lights, and her sexy French-cut red fingernails matched her lip color. She wore a tight-fitting, low-cut, gray wrap dress that accented her bosom, a diamond pendant necklace that sparkled with every move, and black stiletto heels. Lauren was in awe of her beauty.

Mrs. Kenner invited Lauren to sit with them, which she did out of politeness, although it was awkward for her. And so, it was there, sitting across the table from Jack's wife where Lauren wondered how to handle this moral dilemma. She wanted another kiss from Jack, but after meeting his beautiful wife, what chance was there? Why did he even open up that door to her emotions?

While Jack was procuring cocktails and hob-nobbing with co-workers, Lauren got to know a little about Italia. She won a local beauty pageant at one time, which didn't surprise Lauren at all. Despite her poise, she appeared to be rather innocent. She was also soft-spoken, sweet, kind, and funny, and was anxious to learn all about Lauren.

"So, Lauren, what do you do for fun?" Italia asked in her sultry voice.

That was a difficult question to answer. She brought work home almost every night, she watched TV occasionally, and on weekends she did chores and went to the grocery store with a packet of coupons. A pretty routine and boring lifestyle. "Well, I like to go to the movies whenever I can. I like comedies because they make me laugh and get my mind off work. How about you, Italia?"

"I like trying new things. You know, challenge myself. I've been thinking about what to do this summer that I haven't done before," she responded with a twinkle in her eyes.

"Wow! That's impressive." Lauren was quite

surprised at her sense of adventure and her apparent energy. She wondered when was the last time she challenged herself. As a young adult, she thought about hiking the Appalachian Trail, but never did it. She enjoyed painting, but hadn't picked up a paint brush in years. Instead, she focused on what she was good at—processes and organization. That was also what she was paid to do.

Italia suggested, "Maybe there's something we can do together."

"Hmm," Lauren thought. *"That would certainly complicate things."* However, she replied with a smile and a lie, "Sounds like fun."

They exchanged phone numbers.

By the end of the evening, it seemed Italia wanted to be Lauren's very best friend, a title Lauren wasn't so eager to grant. Things were not going the way Lauren imagined them to go. Not at all.

❧ *2* ❧

The morning after the retirement party at the country club, Lauren emptied her clutch bag. There, in the zippered pocket, was a piece of white paper, folded up several times. It revealed a telephone number—Jack's number. Except that it was in Italia's handwriting—feminine and flowing.

"What am I going to do with this?" she thought. *"If I call and Jack answers, what do I say? If Italia answers, what am I getting myself into?"* She couldn't bear the thought of playing along, while her heart ached for Jack.

She left the paper on her dresser, to be ignored indefinitely. She went about her business, both at work and at home, trying to forget about Jack. It wasn't easy. It just made her sadder and lonelier than she had been in years.

However, on the following Thursday night, Italia called Lauren.

"Hey, it's Italia—from the party. I hope you don't mind my calling you. We seemed to hit it off."

"I don't mind," Lauren lied once again. "It's nice to hear from you."

"Want to do something fun this weekend? I thought maybe you and I could go to the beach or catch a movie. What do you think?"

No Jack.

"I...suppose so," Lauren stuttered, while trying to think up an excuse. Now she was committed to this outing. "I suppose if we go to the beach, I could work on my tan, if you could call it that," she continued.

"Great! Beach it is! Where do you want to go?" Italia asked, leaving the choice up to Lauren.

"Um, well, how about Tower Beach? It doesn't usually draw tons of people and they have a lot of great seashells, if you're into that." Lauren knew how dumb that sounded but couldn't take her words back. And she was already wondering how her bathing suit body would look next to Italia's. There really was no comparison.

"Sounds good. Why don't you come over here first, and we can ride together? I can drive," she offered.

Lauren quietly gasped. "Sure," she responded, and wrote down Italia's address. They planned to meet Saturday at 11 a.m. Her stomach was doing somersaults and she felt a little guilty for thinking about Italia's husband. Would he be there and would she be alone with him, even for a minute? Her mind went into overdrive thinking about the possibilities.

Right from the start of her "friendship" with Italia, there was deception on Lauren's part. Her interest was in Jack. She didn't want to "use" Italia as a bridge to see Jack, but in reality, that's what it was. *"How evil is that?"* she thought. It was her hope to have Jack kiss her again. It felt so good, so exciting! She guessed that Jack felt the same way, unless he was just playing with her emotions. So that brought up another scenario. What if he wasn't the good person she assumed him to be? Maybe he was "leading on" several women and she also fell into his snare. She would end up looking like a fool. She'd have to watch for "red flags," before it was too late, like with her ex-husband Phil. What a loser he turned out to be!

When they were married, Phil insisted on managing their finances and bills. Within a short time, he cleaned out her bank account and maxed out every credit card, gambling away the money at the casinos, and leaving a trail of notices from every financial institution they dealt with. On top of that, he watched her like a hawk, making sure she stayed away from family and friends who might question his actions, not allowing her to make purchases in case she'd find out that the credit was turned off, monitoring all her phone calls, and following her wherever she went. Phil always "happened" to be there, too. Lauren couldn't take it anymore. When she started looking into her finances, it hit her like a bomb. She saw a lawyer the next day and filed for divorce and had to start her life all over again. It took her almost ten years to be financially secure. Thank goodness she had a well-paying job!

Proceeding with her plans to meet Italia, Lauren checked the condition of her year-old bathing suit. She tried it on, just in case she needed to buy a new one. It had a red flowery bra and black boy-shorts, and it still flattered her figure. She put it aside with a beach bag packed with sunscreen, a towel, sunglasses, paperback, small purse, and a few dollars for incidental purchases. She also folded up an old blanket for the sand and put it in the trunk of her car.

Saturday came before she knew it. It was a perfect

day for the beach—low 80s and no wind, although there was always an ocean breeze on the beach.

Lauren pulled into the Kenner's driveway and saw a red Miata convertible parked in front of the garage. She wondered if it was Italia's or Jack's. That question was answered when Italia came out and threw her bag in the trunk, leaving it open. She was dressed in "Daisy Duke" shorts and a halter top, tied in the front, showing her deep cleavage.

Italia waved and walked up to her Civic, bending a bit to talk through the open window and revealing more of her cleavage, which Lauren noted. "You can park in front of the other garage door and put your gear in my trunk."

Lauren did as she was told, then glanced around. She didn't see Jack.

"C'mon," Italia said. "I'll give you a quick tour."

The house was a two-story brick colonial with a grand foyer entrance and a massive wooden door. They walked into the foyer. To the right was the living room, which was furnished in a traditional style with a modern, rectangular gas fireplace in a granite wall, and gorgeous hardwood floors. It did not looked lived in. Downstairs there was also a spacious dining room, an open kitchen with dark, ornate cabinetry, quartz countertops and an island, a family room, office, powder room, and double doors to private, serene backyard with a patio and large flower garden. Italia led her up the grand staircase to the second story. There were four large bedrooms and two full, spa-like Italian-marble bathrooms plus one smaller bath in the hallway. Quite a difference from Lauren's modest ranch home with three bedrooms, two baths, and a small yard. Although Italia's home was magnificent, Lauren thought it looked impossible to keep up without a maid and a gardener. She wondered how they could afford such grandeur and if Italia really did housework with her perfectly manicured nails.

Jack came in from the garage, where he had been puttering with his pickup truck. He wiped his hands on a rag. "Hi!" he said with a smile as he spotted Lauren. His white t-shirt and jeans were soiled with grease. "So, you're going to the beach!"

"Yes, girls' day out." Lauren smiled and wanted to say more, but she was uncomfortable, and he looked tentative, too.

"Have a good time." Then, "See you in the office," he added, looking her in the eye. She didn't know whether to read into that or not. She and Italia headed out to the driveway. Jack's eyes followed them out.

Italia jumped into the driver's seat and started the car, and Lauren hopped into the passenger side. Lauren discovered that Italia was not a cautious driver—but more like *Thelma & Louise*. She sped up on curves, ignored speed limits, merged through yields, and did a crawl through stop signs instead of stopping.

Despite a somewhat harrowing 15-mile trip, they arrived at Tower Beach in one piece. They carried their blankets and satchels to the sand and found a quiet spot. There were about fifty other people there, some with children who were screeching louder than the seagulls as they played in the sand and the surf. One tan, muscular male lifeguard was on duty in their section of the beach, blowing his whistle when swimmers went out of the roped area. His voice, billowing through a handheld speaker, carried over the haze to the swimmers.

With her blanket in place, Italia started to remove her outer clothing to reveal a black thong bottom and a tiny swimsuit bra held up by spaghetti straps. Her olive skin was well tanned already and she looked like a goddess. Lauren shed her clothes as well, and felt modest in her more traditional suit. She lathered her pale skin with sunscreen.

Lauren wondered why Jack would kiss her when he had a gorgeous wife like Italia to go home to every night.

Italia ran for the water so Lauren followed. Italia was like a kid, splashing water at Lauren, diving down and grabbing Lauren's ankles until she fell over in the waist-high water, and jumping on her back like a rodeo cowboy! Even though Lauren couldn't help but laugh with her, and had more fun than she had in years, she was relieved when they headed back to the blanket.

Their hair, now soaked, dripped down their backs and faces. Italia dried herself off with a towel, as best she could. She pulled her long black hair to one side.

"Lauren, will you put suntan lotion on my backside?" Italia sweetly asked.

"Sure." Lauren filled her palm with lotion while Italia stretched out on her stomach.

"Undo my bra. I don't want any tan lines there," she requested.

Lauren obeyed, letting the spaghetti straps fall onto the blanket. She started rubbing in the lotion on her shoulders. Italia murmured with pleasure sounds.

"Oh, that feels so good," she gushed.

Lauren spread the lotion around her middle back and felt Italia's large breasts, flattened out a bit by the blanket. They seemed to be real. She continued to her lower spine, her perfectly shaped buttocks, all around her thighs, calves, and feet, and then she was done. Italia appeared to be sleeping, but Lauren wasn't sure. After drying herself off with her towel, she added more sunscreen to her own body, put a rolled-up towel under her head, and went on her back, soaking up the warm sun. She dozed off herself, listening to the sounds of the seagulls.

When she awoke about fifteen minutes later, Italia, still silent in sleep, had her arm around Lauren's waist. She didn't know what to do, so she just left it there. Italia stirred and moved to her back, holding her tiny bra somewhat in place, enough to cover her nipples.

"Lauren, I need more lotion. Could you do my front?" she murmured as she nuzzled into the blanket. "Pretty please?"

"Do you want me to tie your top first?"

"Not yet. No lines. Remember?"

Feeling a bit awkward, Lauren complied, first by dusting off sand, then rubbing lotion all over her exposed skin. She had never touched an almost naked woman before, feeling every curve of her body. It awakened a not totally unwelcome sense of pleasure. When she finished, she was again thinking of Jack and the "need" building up inside. She thought, *"I haven't made love in so long! I haven't felt love in so long! I want it so badly. What am I going to do?"* She knew what she *should* do, but would she? Find someone else? Not an easy task. But, perhaps, a necessary one. She did not want to be a homewrecker. Was she too weak to be strong?

They baked in the sun for another twenty minutes, then brushed the sand off their feet, put their sandals and outer clothes back on, packed up their gear, and headed out. Near the beach, they stopped for something to eat at a roadside burger shack, as they were both very hungry. They carried their greasy meals to a picnic bench, set in the shade of a pin oak tree.

Lauren got a chance to find out more about her while they munched on their burgers. "How long have you and Jack been married?"

Italia dabbed her lips with a paper napkin. "Ten years," she replied. "Have you ever been married?"

"Yes, but it only lasted a few months." Lauren paused, looked back at Italia, then asked, "No children?"

Italia rolled her eyes and quickly answered with a resounding, "No! We decided that, with his work schedule, it would just be too demanding."

Within that message, Lauren was hearing, "...too demanding for me to handle alone."

Lauren spilled out her heart, saying, "I always wanted a family, but it didn't work out that way, and now time is against me." Her eyes looked down in sadness. It was a hard topic to discuss. Then she inquired, "Do you have a large family, Italia? Brothers? Sisters?"

"My parents live in Trenton. No sisters. My brother is in the family business, but he travels a lot."

"So what is the family business?"

"Entertainment sales," she simply said, and then,

"Oh, geez, look at the time!" Italia gasped as she looked at the blue neon clock in the window of the burger shack and took the last sip of Coke from her cup. "I really should get going. I have a mani/pedi in a little over an hour. Today was fun. Thanks for going with me." Italia then added, "It's nice to have a friend." She put her hand on Lauren's and looked genuinely grateful.

"Sure," Lauren replied with a smile, but feeling uncomfortable. "Thanks for driving."

Italia jumped up from the bench and took her trash to the nearest bin as they walked to her car.

Lauren wondered whether Italia had other friends. She seemed very needy and alone. Was she totally dependent on Jack? From what Lauren knew, Italia never held down a job.

"Maybe we can go to the movies next time," Italia offered up as they drove back to her house.

Lauren thought about that for a moment. So, there was to be a "next time." She continued to think about their odd friendship and her feelings for Jack. At what point will something happen? Will she and Jack develop a relationship, or will she put an end to it? Will she continue to befriend Italia, or was that a facade to get closer to Jack? Perhaps she just needed to go back to her old life and forget about both of them. Was that even possible?

"Sounds good. Let me know when," she responded with hesitation.

After all, what could happen at the movies?

3

A shadowy figure leaned against the corner of the building, intently watching two people across the busy avenue. They stood close to one another. The woman smiled and looked up into the man's eyes. The man put his hand on her shoulder in an obvious gesture of intimacy. And then he pulled the woman close, and slowly and passionately kissed her on the lips.

The figure slinked back into the shadows, but continued to watch as the couple parted ways.

Lauren returned to work from George's, a favorite hangout of office workers who needed their liquid lunch or a quick bite to eat.

Feeling elated, she sat at her desk and sighed. She had finally met with Jack. He had stopped by her office that morning and asked if she was free for lunch. She cleared her calendar. During that hour, he never took his eyes off of her. And beautiful eyes they were! Afraid of sounding too dull, she kept the conversation to interesting trips (which were mostly business) and family stories. Jack talked about his truck, his house, and his customers, who were almost all computer nerds. He had to know his product line inside and out to sell to his clients.

Toward the end of lunch, Jack brought up "the kiss."

"I hope you weren't upset with me when I kissed you at the bar that night," he apologized.

"No, no. Not at all. It was...a very pleasant surprise," she responded, blushing. Her heart was beating faster, too.

"It was nice for me, too. I hated to see you leave so quickly. I wanted to get to know you."

Her heart melted.

"I was sorry I had to go, too." She stared into his smiling blue eyes. She could tell it was the correct response. At the time they met, Lauren didn't know that a kiss was coming her way; otherwise, she may have cancelled her ride service and stayed at the bar to get to know Jack. Maybe he would have given her a lift home. Maybe they would have kissed again. Maybe they would have made plans to be together. All these maybes!

She knew that life was all about the choices you make—good ones or bad ones. The history of the world was always determined by someone's choice. Sometimes it led to new scientific findings, the discovery of new worlds, successes in war, and even the birth of a baby meant for greatness. Other times, poor choices led to downfalls of nations, criminal activity, shame, and destruction. In her mind she pictured the Tarot card "The Fool," displaying an upside-down man with a rope around his ankle. She hoped that she was making the right decision by seeing Jack again and would not make a fool of herself.

For now, she had to go down a path that was

unfamiliar and uncertain. There was no process written for ways of the heart. You just had to go with it and enjoy the journey.

"Maybe...sometime...we can do it again," he suggested, placing his hand on hers. She took his hand and held it. It was her way of saying yes, accepting what was to come, whether it was "right" or not. Her heart wanted it, even though her common sense wasn't quite on board yet. She barely knew the man! There was still a long road ahead, but she wanted to walk the walk. She could always change her mind later if she started to see those red flags, or if Italia found out and ended everything. She would have to respect Jack's decision if he backed out of the relationship.

"I'd like that." She didn't want to bring up Italia and break the mood, but Jack did it anyway. He paused for a moment.

"You know, Italia is very fond of you."

"She seems to need a friend," Lauren said with concern.

"Yes..." His mind seemed to wander briefly.

"We're going to the movies on Saturday night. Are you coming with us?"

"Ha! I wasn't invited! That's okay. I have things I have to do that night. You and Italia have a good time."

Lauren paused a moment before inquiring, "Can I ask you a personal question?"

"Sure," he replied but secretly hoped it wasn't too personal. He didn't want to discuss or reveal too much about his marriage.

"You don't wear a wedding ring. Any reason for that?" She looked at him, hoping for a good reason.

"I'm always working on machinery. I don't want to lose a finger or a ring."

Lauren agreed that it was a logical explanation. "Makes sense. Sorry, I just had to know."

With that, he pulled money out of his wallet for the check, stood up, and offered Lauren a hand. She wondered what the "story" was between those two. There had to be one. Perhaps one of them would tell her sometime.

He left her on the corner with a parting kiss. She savored it all the way back to the office.

She had four long hours to focus on the process in front of her, and then she could spend the evening in reverie. She was looking forward to it.

About 3 p.m., a newly hired co-worker, Rennie Nusbaum, stopped in her office.

"Hey, Rennie. What can I do for you?" she inquired.

"I just thought I would stop in and see you. You work too hard," he commiserated with fake concern, as he plopped down in her guest chair.

Lauren thought it was odd that he would suddenly take notice in her work ethic. She assumed that he, as a newcomer, was working on a special project for management. She didn't really know what the project was; it obviously was hush-hush. Rennie was a few years older than Lauren, a little over six feet tall, thin, with pale, white skin, as if he never stepped into the sunshine. His necktie was always loosened around his collar and his shirt sleeves were rolled up. Every morning he propped his suit coat on the back of his chair, never to be worn again until lunch break or quitting time.

She wanted to beg off this conversation. His breath

reeked of whiskey. She figured he hit the bar for lunch. He could have even been at the bar at George's while she was there with Jack.

"I am quite busy," she explained. "Perhaps we could 'chat' another time."

Rennie gave her a disingenuous smile. "We will. For sure," he promised her. He got up from the chair, and pointed an index finger at her, and made two clicking sounds with his tongue.

Lauren wondered what that was all about! She shook her head, mumbled, "Oddball," under her breath, and let it go. She worked with some strange people!

Sue Gainer, the office assistant, popped her head in next. "Everything okay?" she asked. "I saw that creepy Nusbaum in your office."

"Yeah, I'm fine. He wanted to chat; I didn't."

"Well, I know you're busy, so I'll let you get back to work. If you ever need an excuse to get away from that guy, I can call you and say you're needed in the boss' office."

"I'm not worried. But, thanks." Lauren did think that Sue's idea was a good one, so she filed it away in her brain.

Sue smiled and went back to her desk, but she wasn't satisfied. She planned to check out Mr. Nusbaum at her earliest convenience.

When Lauren got home that night, there were two messages on her landline phone recorder, both hang-ups after a moment of silence. She looked at Caller ID, but it just said "Private." It couldn't have been anyone important, she concluded. If they wanted to reach her, they would call back or leave a message.

She spent the evening relaxing, watching TV, and sorting through junk mail. Her thoughts were of Jack's most recent kiss on the street outside George's Bar. Again, it was too short. She wanted more. However, the thrill of the kiss was very special and it made her warm inside. She had forgotten how all-consuming one kiss can be—that moment between two lovers, the longing that follows, perhaps resulting in a passionate encounter. That's what she envisioned; that's what she wanted in her heart.

Thoughts of Italia also went through her mind. What if she found out? What would she do? Lauren hated the thought of hurting her. She was so child-like, so delicate, so needy. It would be a terrible blow. Lauren didn't relish being the "other woman" in Jack's life either. The way things were, she would always take the second spot in his life. That was not what she wanted for her life. Was she willing to wait to become No. 1, if that was even a possibility? Lauren didn't kid herself. Husbands rarely left the security of their marriages. So the answer to that question was no.

And she still wasn't so sure that Jack felt the same way about her. Sure, he kissed her—twice! But she really didn't know him. For all she knew, he could be a serial killer. She laughed at the thought. Of course, Jack was not a serial killer. He was a charming and gentle soul, a career man, a bread winner. She had a momentary thought about "Jack the Ripper." *"No, no, no,"* she dismissed that silly notion.

Lauren also considered the morality of what she was doing. She was never an overly religious person but she thought of herself as ethical. Seeing Jack, kissing Jack, daydreaming of Jack the way she had was not ethical. She knew better than that. It was a moral dilemma and it weighed heavily on her mind. Was she strong enough to resist his charms? She wasn't so sure and that made her feel ashamed.

Her primal urges were taking over. She needed sexual satisfaction. That, at least, was "normal." She also wanted love. The forever kind. And she envisioned that with Jack. Life would be so sweet!

Weary, Lauren climbed into bed. It was time to shut down her mind and get a good night's sleep. As she put her head on her pillow, she wondered if that was even possible. Too many thoughts. Too many desires. What did the future have in store for her? She wished she had a crystal ball. No matter what, it would be much different than her past.

4

Jack awoke on Saturday morning to the smell of sulfur.

"What the...?" He threw off the covers, put on his slippers and a robe, tying it hastily, and went downstairs into a smoky kitchen.

There, on the stovetop, was an exploded egg in a blackened pot, smelling putrid. He turned off the burner, moved the pot to the sink, then opened all the doors and downstairs windows to let out the smoke. He wondered why the smoke alarms did not sound. Italia was nowhere to be found.

He exited the patio door and saw Italia sitting in the garden, completely unaware of the situation inside.

"Italia! You left an egg on the stove! Again!" He was angry. It was the second time she had done this in just the past month.

"Oh. I didn't mean to," she wailed, standing facing him now, and wringing her hands.

Jack sighed. Some days he just didn't know what to do. She was often forgetful and careless. He was afraid she'd burn the house down—with him in it!

"Alright, alright... Please be more careful," he said, forgiving her. "I'm airing out the house."

He went back inside and turned on the ceiling fans to help disperse the smoke. He knew it might take all day to get rid of that smell!

Italia came inside and looked at the pan; it was beyond cleaning.

He had never hit her when he got mad, but she wouldn't put violence past any man. She had seen it before in her own family, when her father hit her mother with a slap of the back of his hand, or worse. Her mother cried and lived in fear and never talked about it to anyone. She always took the hit. But Italia had witnessed it often, and it escalated over time, and she hated her father for it. And her brother was a chip off the old block with his women, too. Memories flooded back into her mind, as well as the rage she still felt in her heart.

Whenever she saw her father strike her mother, she wanted to kill him and even planned it out once, but never carried it through...because she'd lose out on too much. After all, her Papa doted on her, Italia, his "sweet baby girl." If she wanted anything, all she had to do was ask. And she often did. She learned that early in life. "Ask, and thou shalt receive." She took whatever she could, whenever she wanted. Money, jewelry, perfume, clothes, shoes. He kept her in style, insisting that she wear the newest and prettiest clothes, which she always modeled for him. He enjoyed seeing her in heels, even at a young age, walking back and forth in front of him. He would lick his lips and say, *"Bellissimo, bellissimo."*

The only hand her father put on her was a loving hand, perhaps too loving. *"La mia dolce bambina,"* he always called her, petting her long, beautiful hair, squeezing her, and holding her on his lap until she was too big to hold on his lap. He often showed her off to his friends who socialized at their house. They all gave her kisses on the lips and she was obliged to kiss her "uncles" back. They would all laugh. She never quite got the joke, but it made her uncomfortable the older she became.

That morning, Jack hadn't gotten angry enough to hit her. She admitted to herself that she sometimes tempted fate, just to see how far she could push him. Would he be sorry and apologetic and lavish her with love, or gifts, afterwards?

She grabbed a scented spray and walked around the house, spritzing it in each room. Now the house smelled like rotten eggs and tropical flowers.

When the pan had cooled off, Jack disposed of it and what was left of the egg in the garbage tote, wrapping it tight in two plastic bags. Since the egg had exploded, he had to clean remnants from the walls, ceiling, and countertop. It was amazing how far he found pieces of shell. Then he went upstairs to take a shower.

Jack enjoyed his morning routine—a long, hot, steamy shower and shave, and then a quick styling of his hair. It was a quiet time. Alone time. Time to let his mind wander. Time to think of new ideas. Time to organize his day. Since it was Saturday, there was no need to think about work. Instead, he started thinking about meeting Lauren for lunch yesterday. There was just something about her. Yes, she had a great smile and he thoroughly enjoyed discovering her soft lips. But there was something more... He felt quite relaxed with her. She had composure, confidence, and elegance, yet was very alluring, a secret sexiness. He loved the way her hair fell over the side of her face when she moved her head, the loving touch of her hands on his, and, yes, the softness of her breasts, which he got to feel that first morning they "met." He wanted to see her again, get to know her, and perhaps, touch those breasts again.

He was getting a hard-on, which was too apparent to hide, so he quickly wrapped his body with a generous bath towel. It had been a long time since he got turned on and he enjoyed the sensation.

Jack admitted that Italia was good in bed, there was no doubt, but she began to expect something in return. And when she didn't get that something special, she'd pout like a child. It was cute in the beginning when he would write her poetry or leave love messages for her around the house. But that's not what she wanted. She wanted something tangible— like the things her father gave her. Well, he didn't have her father's money to buy gifts every other day, and he didn't understand why she was so insistent about it. He probably fueled the habit himself by buying her everything she wanted when they first met. Now it turned him off and he no longer wanted to keep up the ritual. It was getting old.

Despite their issues, he had everything he needed, really. A good, well-paying job, a beautiful wife, a house with everything a man could want. But he felt dissatisfied with life.

Jack looked at himself in the mirror. He'd never be younger than he was today. Wrinkles were evident, but the mirror lied. It didn't show who he was inside, what was in his brain...or his heart. He still felt twenty-two and fresh out of college, with a youthful exuberance. He had much more to offer and his "damned" life was passing him by. But he didn't know what to do about it. He just knew he had to do something, and that disturbed him.

If he and Italia had children, it would have been more complicated, he surmised. Italia never had any interest in having children. Her model's body was paramount and she spent a great amount of time (and money) taking care of it, from special creams to expensive treatments for certain areas. She, too, was trapped inside an unsatisfying life. What beauty queen can realistically face aging?

Jack remembered when they first met twelve years prior. He had stopped inside a mall and became intrigued by the auditions for a local beauty pageant, and there she was—the most beautiful girl he had ever seen—tall, long-legged, olive-skinned, with shiny black hair flowing down her back, a tiny waist, voluptuous breasts, full red lips, and dark, mysterious eyes. She was wearing skinny blue jeans and a tight white tank top, which showed all her curves. When she walked down the catwalk in her 6-inch high heels, she stopped, looked directly at him and smiled. After the judges interviewed each candidate and cast their votes, she won, hands down, and was on her way to the state level.

As the mall crowd dispersed and disappointed entrants left the area, Italia stayed behind. And so did he. She gave him her number and it was history after that. He followed her to the state pageant, buying her anything she needed—makeup, clothing, even hiring a stylist. Italia was always so "surprised" and pleased at all the attention he gave her. If she asked for more, he gave it to her. He never said no. Just like her Papa. In return, she promised to marry him when the pageants were behind her, and she did. They had a huge ceremony with ice sculptures, white rose bouquets at each table, the best champagne, the most expensive menu, et cetera...and a 14-day honeymoon to Italy, the country of her ancestors. All paid for by Papa.

It was glorious: The romantic gondola ride in Venice, touring the Vatican and tossing coins in the Trevi fountain in Rome, then driving along the western coast and stopping at all the historic towns along the way. It was so exciting to be together, sharing these experiences! But then they had to come home and establish a life, which Italia found to be mundane. She was always looking for excitement, but he had a job that required him to travel from customer to customer, city to city, and sometimes to work long nights. She was lonely. Very lonely. He could see the toll it took on her over the last ten years since their marriage. And on himself. They both were different people now. They rarely had anything in common any more. They hardly ever spoke to each other, even at dinner. The silence was broken only by the clinking of the silverware against the china and the monotonous chewing sounds they both made. Life had to be better than that!

Her sometimes reckless behavior worried him, too. He wondered if her crazy stunts were done on purpose to get his attention. Or were they a cry for help? Or maybe they were meant to cause him harm. Does any married person *really* know their spouse? He could fully understand how a spouse might remain a stranger after ten, twenty, or even fifty years. After all, everyone has a secret. And every spouse holds at least one secret in his or her heart. He wondered what Italia's secret might be.

In the last couple of years he had become this angry person he didn't recognize. Some days he just wanted to walk out, leave everything behind, and not come back. He didn't want to "deal" with all the drama anymore. Perhaps they needed counseling, or a split.

Jack put down his razor and looked at himself in the mirror again. He was leaning towards the split. He might talk to a lawyer in the next week or so. It was time to get the ball rolling, so to speak.

He wiped the last of the shaving cream off his face and styled his hair. There were things he wanted to do today and he was glad that Italia would be off to the movies with Lauren, even though that, in itself, was worrisome. So far, no harm was done, he assumed.

Italia sat in the kitchen, sipping on her coffee and twirling the diamond rings around on her finger. She, too, thought about when she first met Jack. He used to buy her flowers and gifts and take her out to dinner on a regular basis. When was the last time he paid attention to her, in a good way? They hardly ever talked to each other. Jack was always working or puttering with his "damn" truck. He wasn't fun anymore. And he always seemed to be angry. She wanted to have fun, even if she did get a little crazy once in awhile. Despite her delicate demeanor, she was a thrill-seeker at heart and laughed at danger. She didn't mind risking everything for a few minutes driving a speeding car, motorcycle, or boat just to have a little fun.

Fun. That's what she needed. It reminded her of what she told Lauren about challenging herself. It was time to do something different, something exciting, something wild!

She thought about her sex life with Jack. At first it was wonderful, acting out fantasies and having Jack compliment her body and moves. Now, it just wasn't exciting for either one of them anymore. She had been accustomed to more attention than she was getting now. She had a beautiful house, a fast sports car, the huge diamond ring on her finger, and a fat checkbook. But it just wasn't enough! She needed daily adoration.

Much of the need she felt came from her own insecurities. Truthfully, she didn't understand the pain she was feeling or the loneliness. Whatever it was, it was haunting her day in and day out and she couldn't dismiss it. It wouldn't go away. It became an unsurmountable fear of losing everything she possessed, including her own beauty and youth, and that fear was out of control. Italia was sure it had to do with Jack.

Oh, yes, she noticed that beaming smile when he talked to other women from work at company functions. She didn't like it one bit. In fact, she was green with envy and she wanted it to stop. She couldn't force him to stay home, but, once again, she needed the attention on her. At the recent party, she noticed that Lauren was different from the other women. She immediately sat down with her, focused on her, and asked her questions about her life. She didn't seem to be flirting with Jack. She liked that and wanted to spend more time with her. This friendship might really blossom into something special.

This morning Italia tried to focus on what exciting activity she could do to improve the relationship between herself and Jack and to keep him tied to her. What hadn't she tried? Skydiving? Maybe. Bungee-jumping? A good possibility. But would it get Jack's attention? Probably not. He would just tell her to go have fun without him. She'd have to think of *something* they could do together. Something they'd always remember. Something Jack would like to do. Something to draw them together, like they used to be. She sighed. She'd have to give it more thought.

Italia went into the home office and opened the side desk drawer to get a notebook, and there she saw Jack's gun. It was a Smith & Wesson 9mm with a 15-round-plus-1 capacity that Jack had purchased as a self-defense weapon shortly after moving into their home.

"Hmmm," she said aloud. *"Maybe we could go to the gun range,"* she thought. *"Jack would never let me go alone."* She started making her plan. She printed out information on the gun club Jack belonged to and left it by the computer where he would find it. Without a doubt, he'd ask her about it.

Later, when Jack headed for the office, she sat at the kitchen counter and listened for his reaction since she couldn't see him from there. She waited. Nothing happened. She tiptoed over to the office door and peeked in, holding her breath. Sure enough, Jack was looking at the papers.

Jack held the printout on the gun range and became very nervous. *"What the hell does she think she's going to do with a gun?"* he wondered. Stunned, he fell back in his chair to think. He didn't want her messing around with a weapon, as she had no training. He was the only legal one to carry a concealed weapon, not that he did. The gun usually stayed in the desk drawer. Did he dare sign her up for a firearms class or take her to the range? He really didn't want to, especially because she had been so careless lately, if not intentionally trying to cause him harm. It occurred to him that she might use a gun against him some day. *"Well, she could do that without training,"* he concluded. He put the papers back down on the desk and logged into the computer. He did his own search.

Italia was relieved that Jack didn't get angry. He seemed to be considering the idea. She was so happy that she could barely contain herself, but she had to be patient. At least it was something exciting to look forward to. Perhaps it would relieve the stress that both of them had been feeling recently by blasting bullets into a target figure. And she wanted to prove that she could shoot the target right between the eyes!

The movie Lauren and Italia were going to see was a thriller; neither one of them wanted to see a soppy chick flick. Lauren was hesitant to have Italia cry on her shoulder; and Italia just didn't want to be bored. Italia picked the movie and the time. It was the 8 p.m. showing.

Lauren dressed casually in jeans, a coral summer top, sandals, diamond stud earrings, and a simple gold chain around her neck. Italia wore straight jeans, a scoop neckline tee, short boots, hoop earrings, and multiple bangles on her wrist. It was a warm summer night so no sweaters were necessary. They both drove their own cars to the theater and met inside. The tickets were for the upper row so they took the elevator up and slipped into their plush, red recliners. They shared a large popcorn but had their own sodas as they chatted before the previews.

"Guess what?" Italia teased.

"What?"

"I'm going to learn how to shoot a gun! Jack's setting me up with lessons." She wore a big grin.

Taken aback momentarily, Lauren could only ask, "Why?"

"Well, we have a gun and I want to go to the range

to practice. I have to pass a firearms class to get a permit," she explained.

"You live in such a quiet neighborhood; do you really think you'd need to use a gun?" Lauren questioned.

"Maybe not, but you never know these days."

Lauren thought about that for a minute. There was a case, not too long ago, where an older woman walked in during a burglary of her home and was murdered by the intruders. It made a lot of women in their town wary. "Do you have a security system?" she asked.

"We do, but criminals are smart and know how to work around it. Jack told me that. And he's gone a lot so I need to protect myself. Besides, Jack and I can go to the gun range together. It can be a bonding experience!" she beamed. Italia was also proving to Lauren that she and Jack were still a happily married couple.

Lauren frowned a little. She didn't want to hear about them bonding and she felt a little jealous. Just then, the previews started and the noise level increased significantly, causing them to cease their conversation and focus on the screen. That didn't stop Italia from yelling at the characters in the movie.

"No, don't go 'up' the stairs! Get out!"

"Kill him!"

"Kiss her, you fool!"

Luckily, the theater wasn't full and only a few patrons turned around to give her dirty looks or "shush" her. Italia thought it was funny. Lauren couldn't pretend she didn't know Italia. They were the only ones in the back row. She put the tub of popcorn in her face to hide her embarrassment.

Toward the end of the movie, when the scene was tense, Italia took her hand and squeezed it. She didn't let go. It was awkward, but she figured Italia was just involved in the suspense. Italia's hand was soft and warm as it grasped her own hand. Lauren thought about pulling it away, but it was comforting in a friendly sort of way.

When it was over and they were out by their cars, Italia gleefully announced, "I need a drink! Let's go to Casey's down the road for a nightcap."

"Just one. It's getting late," Lauren responded, even though it was Saturday night and there was no need to rush home. She didn't attempt to keep up with Italia, who sped out of the parking lot in her little sports car. She wondered whether a drink was a good idea, but she felt a duty to keep an eye on "innocent" Italia so that she wouldn't get into any trouble.

Casey's was hopping. Lauren could hear the country music booming from inside and a din of voices. A few "buzzed" patrons were leaving the establishment. As quickly as cars left the parking lot, the spots were taken by different cars. Lauren canvassed the lot before finding a spot between two pickup trucks.

Inside Casey's, she found Italia by the bar, already surrounded by three young men, each holding a bottle of beer. They were definitely checking out her body and making lewd remarks.

"Will you look at that booty? Uh huh! She's killin' me," said a guy wearing a black cowboy hat.

"Hey, I saw her first. She's comin' home with me tonight," the second guy corrected.

"My ass. Let's ask her," a muscular guy intervened.

"Hey, honey. Which one of us do you like best?"

At that moment, Italia saw Lauren. "Sorry, guys. I'm here with my girlfriend."

"A lesbo? Damn!" The trio walked away, shaking their heads, dejected.

Italia just laughed. She and Lauren found two empty bar stools and ordered lemon drop martinis, which were popular with the female bar crowd. The bartender did his usual magic by mixing, stirring, and pouring. They both took sips and felt the heat go down their throats.

There was a country band playing at the far end of the bar so they wandered over there. The music was so loud they couldn't hear each other talk. "Where do you want to sit?" Lauren shouted.

"In the corner," Italia replied, pointing to an empty table for two.

It was a dark corner off to the left of the band. Most of the patrons were either at the bar or on the dance floor. They squeezed through the crowd to the table and sat next to each other so that they could both watch everyone else.

After most of her drink was gone, Lauren yelled above the music, "Do you come here a lot?"

"Just here once! I like the excitement of the place. I'll have to come back again. Do you want to come back with me?" She smiled warmly at Lauren. Without waiting for a reply, she looked at her empty glass and called the waitress over.

"As long as it's not a work night!" Lauren smiled back at Italia. Italia nodded. Already she was formulating a plan to make that happen.

A cute blonde wearing white shorts and a black tee

came over to the table. "What can I get you?"

"Two more lemon drop martinis," Italia requested.

"Make that just one," said Lauren. "I have to drive." She didn't want to tell Italia what to do, but she didn't like that she was drinking heavily and driving, especially knowing how she drove her car. The waitress picked up the empty glass and came back with one drink a few minutes later.

"Let's dance!" Italia grabbed Lauren's wrist and pulled her out onto the dance floor. Everyone was dancing in their own style to a fast country tune. Lauren hadn't been on a dance floor in years, but she found it fun (if not funny) as she and Italia made up their own steps and shook their butts, as if they knew what they were doing.

At the end of the song, they were both out of breath and laughing. Italia pulled her close and quickly kissed her on the lips. Stunned, Lauren stopped and looked her in the eyes, questioning what was behind that kiss. Italia just gave her a grin and pulled her back to the table where her drink awaited.

"I think it's time to get you home, Italia," Lauren commented in all seriousness. She grabbed her purse while Italia took two good gulps of her drink.

"I really don't want to go, but I suppose...," she pouted like a spoiled child.

"I'll follow you home," Lauren offered, and led her to the door and out to her car. "Drive the speed limit!" she ordered.

"Okay, okay," she laughed as she started the car. She did as she was told and Lauren drove carefully behind her until they reached Italia's silent street.

They both pulled into the long driveway to Italia's

house, shining their headlights onto the structure. There was a strange black car parked in front of the garage. Italia seemed to recognize it and jumped out of her car.

"Anthony!" she called out. A man stepped out of the black car with his arms open. Italia went up to hug and kiss him. "Anthony, Anthony! What are you doing here?" she cried with glee.

"Hey, Sis!" He hugged her and then looked at Lauren in her car. "Who's your friend?"

"That's Lauren. She's my new best friend! Lauren! Come meet my brother!"

Lauren got out of the car and walked up the mostly dark driveway which was gently lighted by two matching fixtures on either side of the garage. She could hear "peepers" croaking in the distance and watched the flicker of fireflies in the grass. Italia's brother was somewhat stocky, about six foot, with dark features similar to Italia's, well-groomed hair, and wearing a dark jacket, shirt, and jeans, despite the warm summer night. "Hi, I'm Lauren," she greeted.

"Tony." He gave her half a smile, then demanded an answer from his sister. "How come nobody's home? I've been sitting here for half an hour!"

Lauren thought it was curious that Jack was still gone at this late hour.

Italia turned to Lauren, dismissing her. "Thanks for the fun tonight. I'll catch up with you tomorrow." She and Anthony went to the front door while Lauren jumped back in her car and backed out of the driveway. At least Italia was safe and sound. Lauren had a lot to think about on the drive home. Especially the unexpected kiss. *"What was that about?"* she wondered. *"Maybe Italians just like to kiss everyone. Or maybe not."*

S ue Gainer took her usual Saturday morning jog. She found that jogging sent oxygen to her brain and helped her to focus on complex problems. It also gave her the quiet time to think and analyze. When she got home from her run, she'd shower and have a light breakfast to prepare herself for the day. Already she had a plan for what she needed to do today.

She had quite a network of computers, both PC and Mac, two large monitors, a photo-quality printer, and a laser printer at her disposal in the extra room of her apartment in an old Victorian house that she shared with Henry, her new pet hamster, and her lazy four-year-old ginger cat, Butterscotch. Sometimes she'd discuss her findings with Henry, who would excitedly turn his wheel until Sue gave him a carrot to gnaw on. That would keep him busy for awhile. Butterscotch sunned himself in the open window, occasionally stretching his legs and yawning. A warm, gentle breeze drifted in. It was a lovely summer day, but Sue had more important things on her mind than the weather.

Born in Rochester, New York, Sue left behind the brutal winters and took up residency on the east coast to enjoy the sun and sandy beaches and a longer summer. The twenty-four-year-old office assistant was the daughter of a computer programmer father and a math teacher mother, so her logical mind was an inborn trait. She was also driven by justice for crime victims and animals. She volunteered at the no-kill shelter once a week, and worked to find homes for cats and dogs, and posted several pet posters on the bulletin board at work. And she loved a good mystery, fancied herself as a detective, and would like nothing better than to catch "bad guys." But Sue was also a perfect fit in as office assistant in Supply Chain, since she memorized all the processes, what needed to go where and when and by whom. "Efficient" was her middle name.

And it paid her bills.

The downside for Sue was that her mind never shut down. The gears were always turning, and she prided herself with successfully solving difficult problems, even in the middle of the night. Often, she'd jump out of bed and get on her computer because the answer suddenly came to her and she didn't want to forget the solution or wait until morning.

She kept herself slim and trim because she never sat still long enough to gain a pound. Sue wore her long blonde hair in a pony tail most weekends, because it was the easiest way to keep it, but she "cleaned up" really well, transforming herself into a graceful and beautiful young woman when need be.

Sue dated now and then, but it never got serious. That was fine with her since she wasn't ready to settle down. So many things to accomplish! And she wasn't sure she wanted to be tied into a routine: sharing the bathroom in the morning, planning and preparing meals, taking care of kids, and running the kids to their after-school activities. No, that wasn't the life she wanted. At least not right now.

And she didn't want anyone else telling her what to do and when to do it. If she wanted to fly to Florida for a week, she'd just go. If she wanted to play video games, she'd spend the whole weekend in front of her computer. If she wanted to go to the gym and work out, there was no husband to stop her or force her into his agenda.

Today, Sue had her own agenda. She was researching Rennie Nusbaum, and "Reginald" Nusbaum, online. She donned her favorite red Rochester Red Wings baseball cap over her pony tail; for some reason it kept her focused. Then she checked popular social media sites like Facebook, Instagram, and Twitter for Rennie, but he wasn't on any of those, not that he wasn't using a different "handle." She also checked those same sites for co-workers who worked near him, but none of their "friends" or "followers" appeared to be Rennie.

Next, she did a Google search. A lot of Nusbaums, but no Rennie. Then there was a phonebook search, but not very many people still had landlines, including Rennie. She also paid a minimal fee to get public information on him, but came up empty again. Lastly, she looked at Ancestry. There should have been at least a birth record or census data, although he could have been born and lived anywhere in the world. But he didn't seem to exist. *"What the heck?"* she thought.

"Who is this guy?" she asked Henry. Henry looked at her with his beady little eyes without an answer.

Sue decided that she'd have to take a peek at the company's personnel files on Monday. Mr. Beeler kept the drawer locked, but she would check the key number to see if it was one of those standard filing-cabinet key numbers that almost anyone might have.

For now, she was at a dead end. She had hoped to find his home address, at least. Since that didn't happen, and if she couldn't get into the personnel files on Monday, she figured the next step would be to follow Rennie. If he was as sly as she thought he was, she'd have to be careful. She'd have to blend in on the street and in her car. She wished she knew where he might be headed or what was up his sleeve. And how much danger she'd be in. The only thing she knew about Rennie was that he drank whiskey and probably frequented a bar near the office, maybe George's. It didn't make him a criminal, but booze might be an addiction, a weakness. Unless it was made to look that way.

Sue speculated about Rennie's project at the firm. It wasn't announced and she hadn't seen any updated organizational charts with his name. It was odd, indeed. Perhaps he was there to reduce staff, or simply to cut costs, or document some processes, but then Lauren would know about it. You'd think there'd be a rumor, at least. She could only surmise that the president of the company had a special plan that could not be shared with the employees yet. If that were the case, she would resign herself that Rennie was a nobody. Just an average Joe doing an average job. Until then, though, she would tail him whenever she could to find out what he was up to. She just couldn't appear obvious. She had to remain alert. She had to think ahead. She didn't want to be accused of stalking. Or get fired.

Twenty-two-year-old Sheree Ramsey was a single mother of a six-year-old girl who was going to enter first grade in September. She was proud of little Latasha because her reading skills were already that of a second grader. Sheree made sure that Latasha had a new book to read every week. It was important to spend her hard-earned money on the child's education and future. Black students needed all the help they could get.

As for herself, Sheree never finished high school. She knew that she should have—and she wanted to—but she hung around with the wrong crowd and one very handsome, very persuasive football player who led her to the school's darkened goal post one night, stole her innocence, and got her pregnant. She was 16 when Latasha was born and, rather than put her up for adoption, Sheree quit school to care for her. She never expected the father to give her child support. He was young himself and just a one-night stand. After she left school, she never saw him again, although she did read recently that he was picked up, not for a pro-football team, but for possession of a controlled substance. He spent a short time in jail, and was now on parole because it was a first offense.

It was a hard life as a single mother. She sometimes stole diapers and formula from the local Walmart; and after she was "trespassed" from the store, Sheree got talked into prostitution by the neighborhood pimp, "Cash." Things became easier then, as far as an income and her ability to support her daughter, but Sheree wished she had her youth back. Drugs had already taken their toll and made her look older than she really was. They also ate away at her income and getting high was soon the priority in her life. She'd do anything for a high. *Anything.*

Every morning in the summer, Sheree walked Latasha to her mom's house just off Main Street. Sheree's mom, Chantel, would watch her until Sheree came home. Her return was never predictable. Sometimes Sheree would show up at dinner; sometimes it was midnight or later. It depended on how busy the streets were. The weekends were even more unpredictable, as Sheree liked to go to the Fox Den to "party." On those weekends, Chantel kept Latasha until Sunday afternoon when Sheree was sober enough to parent. Chantel never questioned her daughter's schedule or her profession; it was just their way of life.

This particular Saturday evening was no different than the others. Latasha was at her grandmother's house already. It was time for Sheree to make herself sexy. She squeezed into her black-and-white-striped tube top and tight black leather shorts, slipped on her 6-inch-high platform heels, applied her fake eyelashes and long blue fingernails, along with a palette of makeup, made sure her weave was on securely, and packed her "party bag" of condoms, a spoon, glass pipes, butane lighter, pipe stick, steel wool, and other paraphernalia. You never know what you might need. She also stuffed a couple of twenties in her tube top. She looked in the mirror and smacked her thickly coated, painted red lips together, puckering up a kiss to herself. She was hot and she was ready.

The Fox Den didn't get moving till after 10 p.m. She usually took the bus there; she didn't have to change buses and it was cheaper than a taxi or Uber. On the way home, she usually arranged a "ride," whether it was an acquaintance or a "john."

Sheree got off the bus and walked into the bar. She knew all the hired dancers; sometimes they'd all party together in the parking lot after closing. It all depended on what kind of work she had to perform that night. Some johns wanted to take her to a motel, some to a desolate area in a park, and some just wanted to make out in a car in the Den's parking lot.

She grinned and waved to the dancing girls, both white and African-American, who weren't on stage yet and they waved back. The girls already on stage entertained a few men seated at nearby tables who were shouting and whistling with every sensual move the girls made. The dancers were scantily dressed in thongs and pasties and most of them had large implants and curvy bodies. Big butts and breasts. That's what brought in the clientele. Boyfriends and husbands of the dancers were not allowed in the bar while their partners were working. Too often jealous lovers were known to start fights with customers after sexual advances or comments. Roscoe, the owner, couldn't have that. Just wasn't good for business.

Tonight, there were about twelve male patrons at

the bar. No women—although that was no surprise. Sheree recognized most of the men and, going down the line of bar stools, eliminated a few she knew wouldn't buy her a drink or had no interest in partying. She saddled up to a tall black dude they called "Lick," for his history of robberies. He was out of jail, for now.

"Hey, Lick! How's it going?" Sheree asked, batting her false eyelashes.

Lick turned to see who was calling him. "Sheree! Girl, you do look fine," he complimented. "Whatcha want?"

"Beer's good," she said. Sonny, the bartender, was paying attention and plunked a bottle of Dogfish Head on the bar in front of her, then grabbed a few dollars from Lick's stack of bills on the bar.

"You want some action later?" Sheree asked.

"Man, I want to, but my old lady is watching my ass," he informed her. "I shouldn't even be here."

Sheree grunted and moved on. She didn't have time to waste. A couple of other regulars shook their heads. It looked like a bad night. Cash wasn't going to be happy.

It was after midnight when she saw him. A stranger. A white guy with a wad of money on the bar. She walked between him and the dancers, wiggled her behind and waved her arms in the air to the music. When the song ended, she turned to him, looked him in the eye, and smiled with those luscious, big red lips, and blazing white teeth.

"Hey. You're new here. I'm Sheree," she introduced herself.

He was somewhat tall, had dark hair and definitely

a sexy look of approval in his eye. She knew that look. He was already thinking about what he might do to her in the backseat of his car. She had her john.

He let her do all the talking, while he sized her up. She chatted about how she loved to party and asked if he was into ecstasy or crack. She could score some and they could have a good time in the parking lot, if he was interested.

He calmly said, "Sure. How much?"

"Sixty."

He nodded yes.

"Now don't you go away," she teased, as she went over to the pool table where some regulars were playing. Those two twenties came in handy, as she returned with two small plastic bags of tiny white rocks. She'd get sixty dollars from her john, even though she'd have to fork over half to Cash at the end of the night. She was hoping her new john would become a regular. She'd show him a real good time tonight and he'd come back for more.

What she didn't know was that the crack wasn't pure. The pool player had purchased it from some 20-year-old white guy on the corner who "cooked" it himself it with too much baking soda. He used a buddy's car to sell it, not even caring that an angry customer just might go after his friend and kill him. In the drug trade, no one cared about someone else's bad luck. Shit happens.

Sheree, already feeling buzzed, and her john exited the back door of the Fox Den, beers in hand. They went to his vehicle, where she gave him "head." He enjoyed seeing her red lips on his white cock and her black hands pumping it. When he "came," it was one of the best he ever had. Sheree was good at what she did.

Sheree got out her party bag, gave the john her extra pipe, and they started smoking the crack. At the same exact moment, they both started choking and coughing.

"Oh, my God, what is this stuff?" Sheree said as she choked. She looked at her john and knew she was in trouble. After he finished coughing out the foul mix, he had a look of intense rage directed toward her.

"What the fuck are you trying to do to me? Kill me?" he screamed.

"I bought it from 'Sticks' at the pool table," was her excuse. He didn't want to hear any excuses. She knew she had to get away—fast. She grabbed the door handle and tried to open it to escape.

He pulled her back towards him.

She still managed to pry herself free and get out of the vehicle. He jumped out of his door and went around to her side. In her haste to run, she fell on one knee but got back up, screaming and running toward the back of the lot in her 6-inch heels. He caught up with her, grabbed her arm and swung her around. She tried to pull free, but he was too strong. His face was full of malice, as he swung his free fist at her face, smashing her nose and, a second time, lashing those luscious red lips, which were now bleeding profusely.

Then he pulled out a Smith and Wesson 9mm from the back of his pants, pointing it at the side of her head. She saw the gun just for a second, then closed her eyes tight. She knew what was coming next. A bullet to her temple.

It was suddenly quiet in the parking lot. He

glanced around to see if anyone was looking. The music was still blaring inside the bar and no one came running out. He dragged her body to the dumpster, just a few feet away. He lifted her and threw her in head first, with her foot sticking up in the air. He threw his beer bottle in, too.

"Bitch," he said, disgusted.

Sheree never knew her john's name. She never got paid for her services. She never heard the peel of his tires leaving the parking lot. And, alas, she never heard her little Latasha read her newest book at bedtime. It was lights out.

❧ 8 ❧

Lieutenant Mike Fitch was assigned as chief investigator of the murder case of a prostitute behind Roscoe's Fox Den (or just the "Den," as locals called it), a seedy place on a busy thoroughfare. Neon signs for beer and "Girls, Girls, Girls" flashed in their windows. *"More like a den of thieves,"* Fitch thought.

Mike Fitch rose in the ranks from patrol to Sergeant and then to Detective in Investigative Operations after solving two gang murders. Crimes escalated in recent years—drugs, murders, armed robberies—and the police department recognized Fitch's knack for solving them and de-escalating tense domestic situations.

Protocol was always followed by his "gang unit." It had been part of his job to know the repeat offenders, to do homework on prior incidents, to know who lived in the house under investigation and what their habits were, and to effectively make an arrest at a time when they would least expect it. Then the suspect would be cuffed and secured and the house would then be cleared. It was a matter of life and death for his team, who were top-notch officers, to follow training and protocol.

After eight years in Investigative Operations, he was transferred to the Major Crimes Unit, which, for the most part, handled homicides. Mike was given a promotion to Lieutenant. He was well liked and respected by his colleagues and had an 80 percent arrest rate, which was much higher than any other officer in the state of Delaware where the average was only 15 percent.

The call came in at 2:10 a.m. Sunday morning after the Fox Den had closed. Lt. Fitch had been asleep for two hours when the phone rang next to his bed. It meant there was a murder. It was custom for him to shower before bed so he'd be fresh for the next call. He had several shirts and cheap suits hanging in his closet, waiting to be donned perhaps ten times or just once. It always depended on the crime scene.

He arrived at the bar in thirty minutes. There was a team already busy at work on the evidence.

Fitch was hoping to wrap up this case quickly. He always checked the scene himself before getting facts and witness accounts, which could sometimes vary from person to person. He wanted to see the evidence firsthand, and imagine himself in the killer's shoes. It helped him to tie things together.

He walked past the crime-scene tape, which blocked off the entire property, and into the barroom. It smelled of stale beer. A few bottles were still on the bar. Sixteen stools lined the bar, all tattered and taped. There were no CCTV cameras. There was a swinging door going into a dirty kitchen, two dirty restrooms, and a large, metal exit door painted with graffiti going to the parking lot. There was a similar "Employees Only" door going from the kitchen to the outside dumpster. Behind the bar, there was a floor door that led to the cellar, or cooler, where extra cases of beer were stacked. None of the exterior doors had any damage. There was no blood evidence in the bar, either. The till was full.

No robbery.

Fitch proceeded to the dumpster. The CSI team was dusting the outside for fingerprints, and systematically looking for evidence and photographing it, including the placement of the female body. It was untouched and would remain in place until the team finished their process and the coroner arrived, or until Lt. Fitch released it. He looked inside the dumpster and saw that the body was wedged among numerous black trash bags, a broken chair, several-day-old food remnants, and various other trashed items. The team was also photographing the tire skid marks leading out to the main road.

The coroner and his team arrived on scene to retrieve the body. Fitch instructed them to do a rape kit and to test for evidence under her fingernails.

"It's okay to move the body. Pack up the contents of the dumpster," Lt. Fitch told the team. "We'll go through all of it back at the lab." Looking at his detectives, he ordered, "And don't forget the beer bottles on the bar."

The body was placed in a blue body bag on the pavement, away from any possible evidence so that the victim could be identified by the bar owner, examined, and photographed closely.

One of the detectives on scene unzipped the cover of the body bag. Roscoe, the bar owner, leaned over. "Yeah, I know her. Her name is Sheree. Don't know her last name, but she's a working girl, if you know what I mean. My dancers probably know her last name. They all know her, or, er, knew her." The detectives re-zipped the body bag.

The body was also identified by one of the patrol officers in the area as Sheree Ramsey. The 22-year-old girl had been working the streets for four years, according to her rap sheet. Sheree was known for "working" the bar and her drug of choice was crack cocaine. Almost all prostitutes were on some drug, whether heroin, crack cocaine, meth, or ecstasy (which was mostly meth anyway). That's what made them hungry for work, which put money in their pimp's pocket and kept them in line.

It appeared that Sheree had made an unlucky deal or pissed off a "john" in the wee hours of Sunday. Lt. Fitch said aloud to himself, "What did you do to piss this guy off?" He then examined at the body and could see an obvious gunshot wound to the temple, close range. He could tell by the stippling on her scalp. She had to know death was coming, although she may not have had time to do anything about it. It was a through-and-through, with pieces of skull missing on her left side. From the scene, he also knew that she was killed in the parking lot, as the blood and brain matter on the pavement told the story. The blood evidence was marked with a forensic yellow a-frame number 1, which had been photographed by the CSI team. Her blood left a trail going to the dumpster, so she had to have been dragged. The brain matter was collected for later examination. Smelly stuff, that brain matter.

A small plastic bag with residue was also retrieved

as evidence.

No gun was found but there was a casing. Fitch envisioned the crime. The killer was most likely right-handed and grabbed her right arm with his left hand, putting the gun to her right temple, and pulling the trigger. After she was shot, she was ditched into the dumpster, like yesterday's news. *"Had to be a strong guy,"* Fitch thought, *"to lift and toss her body."*

The bar owner, Roscoe DiNatale, had nothing more to offer. He knew nothing; he saw nothing. Lt. Fitch told the officers to take him to headquarters to be questioned, which they did. Mike would interrogate Roscoe himself later.

"Who called 911?" Lt. Fitch asked the detective at his side.

"Bartender. He was taking trash out to the dumpster when he saw a foot. Ran back inside and called."

"Let's get his statement. Oh, and get a copy of that 911 tape." After a brief pause, he added, "Find out who her pimp is, too."

Fitch asked his detectives to canvass the street, knock on doors, find out if anyone saw or heard anything, check for surveillance cameras, and talk to the street girls for any suspicious johns who may have threatened them or creeped them out.

"I'm going back to the station. Let me know if you get any leads." Two detectives nodded, decided on their routes, and then took off to find some witnesses.

Fitch headed to his car through a throng of several TV cameras and reporters, all yelling at the same time, "What can you tell us about what happened here tonight?" To every reporter he replied, "No comment."

He knew that the suspect may have been a frequent patron of the bar. First and foremost, he had to get the names of those patrons, and each one had to be questioned, even if they had to do it at their doorstep. All of them had to have their arrest records checked. It was going to be a long night.

Roscoe was in Interrogation Room 1, where the walls were heavily padded for those angry or mentally unstable suspects. There were three uncomfortable metal chairs at the small table—one against the side wall and two across. Roscoe had his head down on the table when Lt. Fitch unlocked the door and walked in. He sat down across from Roscoe.

"Okay, Roscoe, suppose you tell me what you know about what happened tonight." Fitch started taking notes, even though the statement was recorded. Detective Al White watched on a monitor in a side room.

"Hey, I was in my establishment all night. I didn't see anything." Roscoe's right hand pushed back his thinning dark hair. He wanted to get this over with, as he was tired and wanted to go home. He had to open up the bar at 7 a.m. for the early-bird regulars—a bunch of old guys who just wanted camaraderie, beer, a shot or two (or just coffee), and plenty of lottery scratch-offs. Roscoe needed some sleep.

"Did you hear a gunshot?"

"Nah. The music was playing loud."

"So, you're saying the gun was fired before closing time," Fitch asked, trying to pin down the facts.

"No! I don't know. I didn't hear anything," Roscoe replied defensively. "I didn't hear no gunshots!"

The detective pressed on. "Did you hear anyone

screaming?"

"No! Nothing, I tell ya."

"How about the cars in your parking lot? Did you see any unusual activity or any unfamiliar cars in your lot?"

"I never went out there from the time I got to the bar to the time you guys arrived," Roscoe explained.

"Not even to take a peek at the body in your dumpster when your bartender called 911?"

"I know better. I've been 'around the block' a few times," Roscoe admitted. "Besides, I had a business to run."

"After closing?" Fitch said, suspiciously.

"There's always clean-up and taking care of the till," Roscoe responded.

Fitch wasn't getting anything useful out of Roscoe. "Who was in your bar tonight? I want names. And the names of your dancers. Here's a tablet. Write 'em down."

As Roscoe started a list, Lt. Fitch had a second thought. "Did anyone pay by credit card tonight?"

"Ask the bartender, Sonny. I never got around to looking at the till. I usually count the cash and deposit it at the Chase Bank on my way home. I hope no one steals my money while I'm here!" Roscoe complained.

"There was a 22-year-old girl dead in your dumpster and you're worried about a lousy $200?" Mike gave him a disgusted look. "Keep writing. I'll be back." He stood up and left Room 1, locking it behind him.

After checking with his detectives, he did not receive any new leads. He unlocked Room 1 and went back in.

Roscoe put down the pen. "There was one guy I never saw before. Dark hair. About 5 feet, 10 inches tall. Had one beer and left."

"Write it down." Roscoe scribbled a few more words and then Fitch released him.

Next, Sonny, the bartender, was brought into the same room Roscoe had just left. He gave Fitch similar information. *"At least their stories match,"* Mike thought. No credit cards were used. That made it tougher. He said the unknown guy ordered a Corona beer with a lime, which was unusual for that establishment. The local beers were ordered most of the time. Fitch noted it. He would check with the lab eventually to see if they had the empty bottle and if there were fingerprints.

While his detectives were searching records on the patrons and dancers, Fitch decided to pay the coroner a visit. He went to the morgue where he was greeted by a man in a white coat, blue gloves, cap with a plastic eye shield, and blue booties.

"Hey, Mike. How's it going?" the doctor asked the lieutenant.

"You tell me, Bob!" Fitch responded. "What do you have?"

"Well, as you know, there was a casing." Coroner Bob Anderson told Fitch, "The team also located the bullet. 9mm."

Pointing to the victim's head on the autopsy table, he continued, "One shot to the right temple, close range. Through and through." Then he moved on to her other injuries. "Broken nose. Face and lip contusions. She must have been hit in the face at least twice. White residue in her mouth and throat. Bruise on the upper right arm. Abrasions on the right knee with gravel in the wound. That's all I can tell you now. Have to wait for the toxicology results. It could take awhile."

Fitch wasn't surprised with the autopsy results or the wait for toxicology. It was the bullet he needed as soon as possible. "We need that bullet to compare to the gun when we find it," he stated.

Using tongs, the coroner dropped it into an evidence bag, sealed it, marked it, and handed it to the lieutenant. "It's been recorded and photographed." The coroner grinned as he handed the bag to Fitch.

"Thanks, Bob. Let me know when you get anything more."

"You know I will." Bob turned and started work on his next autopsy before Fitch even left the morgue.

Dawn was breaking. Before Mike went back to headquarters, he went to the home of Chantel Ramsey to do the death notification. As expected, it was extremely difficult for the family and for him. Sheree's little daughter was just getting out of bed and rubbing her eyes. Mike's heart broke that this sleepy little girl would no longer have a mother. She might not even remember her mother as the years went on. And it would be hard on Sheree's mother as well, having to raise a child by herself at her age.

"Do you know of anyone who would want to cause harm to your daughter?" Mike asked.

Chantel replied through her tears, "I know she led a dangerous life, but she was a good mother. She loved her little girl! I don't know anyone who would want to kill her." She sobbed some more.

"As soon as we find the person who did this, we'll

let you know.”

“Thank you,” Chantel said as she dabbed her eyes with a tissue.

He stood up to leave but Little Latasha walked over to him. “Do you want me to read you a story?” She showed her book to him.

“Sure. That would be nice,” he said. Latasha climbed into his lap and read the children’s book about a lost puppy from beginning to end. Mike thanked her and said she did a great job. Latasha smiled and ran into another room.

Mike let himself out. He sat in his car for a few minutes thinking about that little girl. He was determined to find who did this to her mother!

Back at his desk at police headquarters, Mike felt tired, but that wasn’t unusual. Most of his calls came in the middle of the night when the bars closed. He poured some strong, black coffee into his oversized mug and took a satisfying sip. He kept protein bars, the kind with nuts and caramel, in his desk just for nights like this. He grabbed one and ate it with his coffee.

His lead detective, Al White, knocked on his door.

“What do you have?” Mike was hopeful.

White gave him a thumbs up. “We didn’t find the Corona bottle on the bar, but there was one in the dumpster with the lime still inside. The lab has it now. It will take a day or two for fingerprints and longer for DNA.”

“Good work, Al.”

At least they had something to go on.

❧ 9 ❧

On Monday morning, Sue arrived early to work. She parked her car where she could see who was driving in and what kind of car they owned. At five minutes to eight, Rennie showed up in an old maroon Ford Crown Victoria and parked at the end of the lot and at the end of the row. He got out, dressed in a suit and tie, opened the wide, rear driver's-side door, grabbed a briefcase from the back seat, and headed for the office door. Once he was inside the building, Sue got out of her blue Toyota Corolla and walked, as fast as she could, to Rennie's car. She checked her surroundings to make sure no one was paying attention to her movements. She knew she was probably on surveillance video but, unless someone complained, it wouldn't be an issue. Sue got out her phone and snapped a picture of Rennie's tag. She looked around again, then took a quick look inside his car. Clean as a whistle. The only two items she spotted were a remote for a garage door clipped to the visor and a thermos sitting in the console. She walked back to the building and to her office.

After getting settled at her desk, she went to the break room for coffee. There was Rennie, filling a ceramic mug, printed with the company logo, with black coffee from the freshly brewed pot. She didn't speak to him, and he didn't even look at her. She watched him return to his desk. Unfortunately, his office was near Mr. Beeler's door. She'd have to wait if she wanted to snoop.

At 11:45 a.m. Rennie donned his suit coat and went out for lunch, probably a liquid lunch, based on his usual afternoon breath. Mr. Beeler, a tall, gray-haired man in a crisp tan suit, left a few minutes later, closing his office door behind him. By noon, most of the department was empty except for a few reps taking calls in their Customer Service area. They had better things to do than watch her.

She casually walked by Mr. Beeler's door and tried the knob. It opened. The spacious office was dark, as the floor-length curtains were closed and his large beige ceramic lamps were turned off. Sue tried to open the filing cabinet but it was locked. She didn't want to turn the lights on and attract attention, so she used the light on her cell phone to look at the keyhole. She heard some voices, so she cut the light until the voices drifted away. Lighting up the keyhole in the cabinet again, she saw that the key was S-105, a widely used key. "Yes!" she whispered with satisfaction. After peeking out the door and looking up and down the hallway, she slipped out of the office.

Sue went back to her own office and looked through her key ring. She had an S-105 key. She decided to wait until after hours to go back because Mr. Beeler might come back soon. She didn't have access to his online calendar; only his personal secretary did.

Her hands were trembling from the unauthorized

search of Mr. Beeler's office. She rubbed her hands together and decided to eat lunch at her desk. She pulled a newspaper out of her tote and started reading, while munching on her ham and cheese sandwich. Robberies, shootings, overdoses, court cases, employment issues, national and local politics, and editorials were all covered in the first section. One article caught her eye because of her interest in crime. A prostitute was found dead in a dumpster behind a local bar early Sunday morning. Chilling! She wondered if it was drug related. Everything seemed to be these days. The victim was only twenty-two years old. Somebody's daughter. How horrible!

Discarding her lunch trash, Sue went back to work for four hours until everyone (except Customer Service) was done for the day. Nusbaum was out the door by five; Mr. Beeler didn't leave until six. It was quiet now, except for the occasional ring of a phone on the other side of the building.

Stealthily, Sue went to Mr. Beeler's door with the cabinet key in hand. The door was locked! It was quite frustrating for her. She decided to check out Rennie's office. Just like his car, his office was clean as a whistle. His desk was locked. There were no papers on his desk, no phone memos, not even a doodle on his notepad. She returned to her office, put the key in a cup on her desk, and left for the day. There wasn't anything more she could do there.

Plan B was to drive to some of the nearby bars, which she did. The first stop was a popular seafood restaurant, The Blue Whale. She cruised the parking lot but didn't see Rennie's car. When she got to the second stop—George's—the maroon Crown Vic was in the rear parking lot. She put her hair into a pony tail, put on her cap, and went inside. Rennie was sitting at the bar, watching the news on a large-screen TV. He had a shot of whiskey and a beer chaser in front of him. He didn't turn around to see her entrance. Sue found a booth with a decent view of the bar. She ordered ginger ale, then another, until Rennie got up to leave. She turned her body around and tipped her red baseball cap lid down so that he wouldn't recognize her. He didn't seem to. At least he didn't look at her or speak to her.

She left the bar, giving Rennie time to get to his car. From the shadows, she watched him get into the Crown Vic. As soon as she could, Sue jumped in her own car and casually followed him through town, staying back far enough to be unrecognized. Unfortunately for Sue, Rennie spotted the tail within a block of George's. He watched her in his rear-view mirror and drove around aimlessly for a few blocks, planning to either ditch her or confront her. Rennie didn't want to be questioned, so he turned a corner and drove into an alley as quickly as he could with his large sedan, driving around a building and keeping his car out of sight until she drove by.

He had a problem on his hands and her name was Sue.

❧ *10* ❧

On the following Saturday, Jack and Italia planned to go to the gun range. They both got up early, showered, dressed, and had breakfast. Just before they headed out the door, Jack went to get his gun. It was in a slightly different place than where he left it in the desk drawer.

"I wish Italia wouldn't mess around with my gun until she can handle it!" he thought. He felt himself getting red with anger. However, in just a short time they'd be going over all the information and he or the instructor would familiarize her with his gun. So, he let his anger go.

Today, they were shooting inside. Jack was buying ammo there, as well as the paper targets and any other accessories they'd need. Italia had an instructor, Ray, who was going over the basic rules with her. They both donned in-ear and on-ear muffs to reduce the intense noise and goggles for eye protection.

Ray showed her how to position herself and hold the gun. "The gun isn't loaded right now," he began. "This is the way I want you to stand. Watch me." Italia paid attention. "Put your feet apart, just a little wider than your shoulders and then move your strongest leg back a couple of inches. That way you won't rock in recoil. Hold the gun in front of you with two hands and grip it as tight as you can. That's important, because you don't want the gun to move up or down when you pull the trigger. See the target in your lane? That's what you're going to shoot at today. But don't worry about aiming right now. Relax your knees and elbows so they are slightly bent. Point the gun at the target. Now you try it."

She moved into the position and Ray made sure her stance was correct and that she was holding the gun tightly.

"Now pull the trigger, without moving the gun."

Click.

"Go ahead and pull the trigger a few more times to get the feel of it."

Click, click, click.

"Good."

"Never load your gun until you're ready to shoot and make sure the muzzle is pointed down when you're loading. Also, keep it pointed down until you're ready to shoot," Ray warned, "but be careful not to shoot the floor because the bullet can ricochet."

"Got it," Italia said.

"Okay, let me show you how to load the magazine." Ray paused while he showed her and gave her an opportunity to try it. He also showed her the slide and explained the trigger reset.

"Now stay close to the firing line. Don't put your finger on the trigger until the target is in place and you're ready to shoot. And don't move forward of the firing line. Have any questions?"

"How many bullets do I have?" Italia asked.

"Good question. You have a 15-plus-1 gun, so 16.

When we loaded your gun, we put the magazine in once, which loads the first round in the chamber. Then we removed the magazine and added the extra bullet to the clip, so now you have 16. Anything else?"

Satisfied, she said, "No. I'm ready to shoot."

"Okay, hold that gun tight. Finger on the trigger, and squeeze once."

BAM! The force was more than she expected, but her stance kept her stable. Her bullet hit the target, but not the head. She adjusted the height of her gun and shot again. BAM! This time she hit the head. BAM! The third time was a charm. The bullet hit the target right between the eyes!

"Good, good," congratulated Ray. "With a little bit of practice, you'll be a natural." He smiled at her and she smiled back, pleased with herself.

She continued firing until she used up her ammo. She felt proud of herself and it gave her a sense of empowerment, which she relished.

Jack was surprised at how well she performed. He found it more than a little unnerving. She was far too good her first time at the range.

Italia put the gun back in the case and gave it to Jack. At that point, he did some target shooting before they called it a day and cleaned up their area.

Italia still had to attend a class to get her permit, but it was held only once a month. Then they would come back to the gun range and, hopefully, she would remember what she learned today. He might even buy her a gun so that she'd leave his alone. *"Perhaps it's a good idea,"* he thought, *"to protect herself while I'm out of town or she's alone."* For those few minutes, Jack had forgotten that he was considering divorce. It was difficult for him to imagine living separately, even though that was his ultimate goal.

As they went out to the parking lot, a lone figure remained in the range. With a pair of gloves, he picked up one of the spent bullets and put it in a white envelope, sealed it, and marked it.

$$\approx 11 \approx$$

The phone in Lauren's living room rang late on Saturday afternoon. Caller ID said "Private." She picked it up on the second ring. She hoped it might be Jack—or even Italia.

"Hey," the familiar voice said. She recognized it immediately as her ex-husband Phil.

"Oh, it's you. Why are *you* calling?" Lauren asked in frustration. "Money again?" she guessed.

"I need five hundred bucks. I got guys on my back."

The "guys" who were after Phil were not casual poker friends or even casino operators. They were cold, hard criminals who ran a gambling ring out of a phony corporation and they meant business in more ways than one. The company accepted online bets from customers, including Phil, through multiple websites after they had used a secret login to access those sites, which were located on the dark web, an encrypted network between hidden servers and their listed clients. When Phil's credit evaporated, the debt collectors started to threaten him for money due. He sold his TV and computer, but it still wasn't enough to pay back the debt that mounted daily. He needed more money, fast, and he knew he could get it from his ex. It was an addiction for Phil, so he schemed and begged whenever he needed more money to satisfy his gambling urges.

"You work! Get it yourself! I'm done!" she shouted into the phone.

"Hey, hey, hey. Don't get grumpy. I wouldn't ask if I didn't need it. And I know you're good for it."

"I've got bills, too," Lauren shouted back at him.

"Oh, like for that nice party dress you bought recently?" he taunted.

Lauren gasped. He was still watching her.

"That's none of your business," she replied with anger, but, in reality, she was shaking.

"Oh, I know what you've been up to with that guy from your office. Do you think I'm stupid?" This time Phil was angry—and jealous. "What if I tell his wife?" he threatened. "How would you like that?"

Again, Lauren gasped. She didn't respond right away. How much did he know about Jack and Italia? And her connection with both of them? What didn't he know? As if reading her mind, Phil started laughing. "So, how about that five hundred bucks now?"

She hung up, feeling shock and fear.

She had no idea where he was calling from. Most likely he was within sight of her house so that he could pick up the money. She made sure her doors and windows were locked and turned off the TV and lights. She grabbed her cell phone and went into the bathroom, locked the door, and sat on the commode lid. She heard the landline ringing again. It rang and rang countless times before it stopped. Then it rang again about twenty times. When it stopped, she slipped out of the bathroom and removed the cord connector from the wall, then escaped to the bathroom again. But he knew she was home, and she knew he was out there. As a last resort, she'd call 911. She just didn't want to bring Jack and Italia into it, but Phil might. He was already holding it over her head. Blackmail!

"What have I gotten myself into?" she wondered. *"I should have known better!"* Lauren was trembling. She didn't want to stay in the bathroom all night, nor did she dare to fall asleep in her bed. When things seemed to be quiet, she went into bed but stared at the ceiling most of the night. *"Maybe I should give him the five hundred bucks to get him out of my hair,"* she considered. She knew he'd be back again, though. "He'll never go away until he's dead! Or I'm dead." she said out loud. Perhaps the guys who were looking for him would catch up to him. Immediately she felt guilty for wishing him dead. She just wanted him out of her life, for good!

On Sunday morning, Lauren hooked the phone connector back into the wall, expecting the phone to ring. It didn't. She sighed. Maybe he left and got the money from someone else.

It was troubling to know, though, that he was watching her every move. When had he seen her with Jack? In the bar? On the street? There really wasn't much to worry about. She and Jack had simply kissed, although it was more than a peck. The second kiss, she remembered fondly, was accompanied by a long embrace. It may have appeared innocent to passers-by. But anyone could have seen them on the street. She had to be more careful. It was folly to think they wouldn't be recognized.

Had he seen her with Italia, too? Could he have

seen Italia kiss her at Casey's bar? There was such a crowd there, he could have been ten feet away and she never would have seen him. Phil seemed to be aware of only Jack, so Lauren was less worried about Italia and her flirtations.

Lauren checked her online banking statement to make sure Phil hadn't gained access. She wouldn't put it past him to try. She changed the passwords for several accounts and put her credit on hold.

She was actually surprised that she hadn't heard from Phil by the end of the day. *"What is he up to?"* she thought nervously. She peeked outside the curtains that hung ceiling to floor in her living room, but there was no figure pacing the street or sitting in a parked car. She was sure he'd resurface one of these days. Just not today.

* * * * *

Phil wanted revenge for Lauren hanging up on him. He was pissed and he needed that money! He could have lingered outside her house and intimidated her, but he had to get his hands on the cash right away and she was obviously not going to give it to him.

So, on Sunday morning, he went to the next best source. The Kenners. Using his cell phone, he looked up their address on the internet. Boom! There it was. Next, he typed in Driving Directions. Only ten minutes away. Easy-peasy.

"Pretty nice house!" he said, talking aloud to himself as he admired the large, well-maintained property. "I think I just hit the jackpot!" He sat in his car and watched the house for awhile, to see who was coming and going. He saw two men, both with dark hair, but one was a little more stocky. He wasn't Lauren's lover. It was the slimmer guy. He made sure "Mr. Slim Jim" was alone before he approached.

Phil walked up to Jack as he was hosing suds off his truck, and greeted him in a friendly, upbeat manner, "Hey. You must be Mr. Kenner!"

Jack turned around to see this stranger in his driveway. "Morning. Do I know you?"

"I'm sure you heard of me. I'm Phil, Lauren's husband, or should I say, 'ex.'"

Jack didn't know what to say, so he said nothing, at first. Lauren may have mentioned his name, but he didn't remember. They just stared at each other in the eye. Jack's voice turned cool, "So, what do you want, *Phil?*"

"Hey, look. I'm not here to cause any trouble, *Jack,* but I know you've been, let's say, somewhat friendly with my ex. I can go away quietly for $500 and your wife will never know."

This shocked Jack, but he tried not to show it. His heart was beating rapidly in his chest. He stared into Phil's eyes and thought about it for a long while. If he gave Phil the money, he'd go away, hopefully forever. If he didn't give Phil the money, Phil might be brazen enough to tell Italia all about the kiss or kisses that he shared with Lauren. That would lead to a conversation he was not ready to have, especially with Tony present in his home. It might even lead to something more sinister.

Jack gave in. "Alright. But you'd better not show your face around here again. And leave Lauren alone."

Phil broke him down. "Sure, man, sure," he agreed with a grin...and a lie.

Jack put the hose down, went in the house, and returned a few minutes later, handing over the cash to Phil, who pocketed it immediately with a big smile. Phil also saw the stocky man standing in the doorway. He didn't like the looks of him; he looked like kind of guy who was looking for him. Phil left, feeling full of glee that he had his money. It would tide him over for a little bit. Would he hand it over to the guy he owed? Maybe. Maybe not. Maybe there was more money to be made here.

Jack watched Phil back his rusty Buick out of the driveway. He took a mental picture of the vehicle in case Phil decided to blackmail them for more money. He couldn't risk it for Lauren or himself. There was too much at stake.

Unhappy about the entire transaction, Jack felt "taken." This guy Phil was trouble. He certainly didn't want Italia to know. But there was big-mouth Tony standing in the door between the garage and the house, waiting for Jack to come inside. He didn't have a friendly look on his face.

"Who was that asshole?" Tony asked menacingly. A vein popped up over his brow as he clenched his teeth.

"Nobody you need to know," Jack replied, pushing Tony aside with his shoulder. Tony wasn't used to being at the receiving end of a shove; it was usually the other way around. His anger only intensified.

Tony argued, "If it concerns Italia, it is my business." He formed a fist with his right hand, ready to use it with the slightest provocation.

"Tony, I know you're Italia's brother and you want to look out for her, but it's really none of your business," Jack explained, with no intention of providing any more information.

"I'll make it my business," Tony threatened. He never liked Jack to begin with, and he liked him even less at this moment.

"This is my house..." Jack corrected, "...er, our house, and perhaps you've overstayed your welcome, if you know what I mean." His tone was serious and firm. Once again, Tony was not used to a bold confrontation from "some asshole" like Jack, but he was his sister's husband. He used great restraint with both his words and his fist.

"You don't know who you're talking to," Tony retorted, defiantly, with his chest bumping into Jack's and pointing his finger in Jack's eye.

Jack put his foot down. "One more week. That's it!" Jack walked past Tony and into the kitchen. He had had enough of his B.S.

"We'll see about that, wise guy. I think Italia will have something to say about it," Tony shouted at Jack's back.

Tony stormed off to find Italia. Jack hoped it got his mind off Lauren's ex.

Since Italia never pursued Jack with questions about Lauren's ex, Jack assumed that Tony never mentioned the visit to her. Tony's biggest concern was apparently his free stay at their house. *Doesn't anyone miss him at the business?* Jack wondered. He just let it go. Hopefully, Tony would head back to New Jersey shortly and be out of their hair. It couldn't happen fast enough.

Meanwhile, he wondered how Phil knew who he was and how he found him. He would have to talk to Lauren. Alone. Away from the office and eavesdropping ears. He didn't want to discuss it in e-mail either. He planned to ask Lauren out for lunch.

Jack went back to washing his truck, but his mind was elsewhere. What if Phil came back for more money? What if he wasn't home and Phil said something to Italia about Lauren? Now he was worried. What started as just an "innocent" kiss goodbye in a bar may have led to something troublesome, something dangerous, perhaps something life-threatening. Definitely life-changing. This wasn't what he bargained for. He thought he could have a secret relationship with Lauren and no one would be any wiser. Now, it seemed, the worst kind of person—a blackmailer—knew the details of at least one of their encounters including the fact that he was a married man. He really did not want Italia to find out and he would take *any* steps necessary to stop Phil from spreading malicious tales, even though they may be true. *"Is it too late to go back in time? Yes,"* Jack thought. *"It is."*

❧ *12* ❧

Lauren was spending a quiet evening at home, the night after Phil harassed her. After putting on a Josh Groban CD, she poured herself a glass of merlot, polished her nails, let them dry, then got ready for bed. In a box from the store was the new green silk nightgown with the spaghetti straps that she bought right after she met Jack, hoping she'd get to model it for him. Unsure that she would ever wear it for him, she decided to put it on tonight. At least she would get some use out of it.

Wearing the nightgown, she looked at herself in the mirror, turning in every direction. It showed off her bosom, slim waist, and lovely white back, giving her an exotic look. *"Too bad Jack may never see me in it,"* she thought. She had almost given up hope, and now she had an additional worry that Phil would see them together and she couldn't allow that.

When the doorbell rang, it made her jump. "Who is it?" she asked loudly, hoping it wasn't Phil again.

"Italia!" came the all-too-familiar voice on the other side of the door.

"Italia? What is she doing here?" Lauren thought with relief as she walked to the front door. "Coming!" she called out.

She unbolted the lock and opened the door. There was Italia with a big grin on her face and wearing scanty white shorts and a navy halter top. "Surprise!" she exclaimed. Lauren was glad to see her and gave her a big smile back. Italia was the one who got the biggest surprise, though, when she saw Lauren in the slinky nightgown.

"Come on in," Lauren invited. "I was just getting ready for bed."

"I can see that. I thought I would just stop by to say hello. I was feeling kind of lonely. Jack is off somewhere again and Anthony said he was going drinking with old friends. So, here I am." She walked in and looked around at the modest surroundings. "Show me around," she suggested.

"Before we do, would you like a glass of merlot?"

"Sounds good."

Lauren poured another glass of wine and handed it to Italia. "Cheers," they both said, clinking their glasses and taking a long sip. Lauren finished what was left in her glass and poured a little more.

"Okay," Italia said, while placing her glass on the kitchen counter. "How about that tour?"

"Well, there's not much to show. The kitchen and living room are 'open concept,' as you see. There are three bedrooms—one I use for my computer room." She led Italia through the open door where Italia took a quick look and nodded in approval. "Guest room is over here." She took her down the hallway to the room. There was a queen-size bed covered with a country quilt, a tall-boy dresser and two night stands with matching lamps. Continuing the tour, she recited, "Guest bath, linen closet, laundry room, door to the garage, and door to the basement, and lastly, my bedroom with its own bathroom. It looks out at the back yard."

"So, this is where the magic happens," Italia laughed as she looked around the feminine-styled room with a flowered bedspread and lacy, white pillow covers.

"I wish!" Lauren laughed, too.

Italia turned serious. She pulled Lauren to her body, held her face in her hands, and, while closing her eyes, passionately kissed her on the lips. Immediately, Lauren felt immersed in Italia's passion, put her arms around her, and returned the kiss. The wine that Lauren drank relaxed her and left her open to Italia's advances. Italia's lips were soft and supple. She smelled of expensive perfume. Her long, black hair cascaded down Lauren's bare shoulder. As they held each other in a loving embrace, Italia's hands started to wander down to Lauren's breast, finding her aroused nipple through the silk nightgown. It gave Lauren a "start." She wasn't expecting that.

"Let's go to the bed. Please," Italia begged softly, as she switched off the light. She kissed Lauren again, more gently this time.

Lauren remembered adding lotion to Italia's body on the beach and how beautiful she looked and how she felt when she touched her skin and her breasts. She had a strong urge to do whatever Italia wanted, because she wanted it, too. But suddenly she had a thought of Jack and that's where she wanted her life to go—with him, not with his wife! She broke the embrace.

"Italia. Stop. Listen. I am very fond of you. You are

turning me on, I won't lie. But I like men."

"I like men, too, but I really need you right now," she continued to plead. She gently pushed Lauren onto the bed in the darkened room, and, after kicking off her sandals, straddled her. "Please, Lauren. I won't hurt you. I love you. Don't you feel the excitement as our bodies touch? Don't you want to be caressed from head to toe? I know I do. I've wanted to kiss you and touch you for weeks. You are so beautiful." She kissed Lauren's shoulder, causing the strap to dangle. Then she kissed her breast through the nightgown, and then her stomach, and then the soft mound beneath her bellybutton.

Lauren was losing the battle. She felt herself wanting more, desiring Italia's touch. In her mind, she knew she must stop this, but her body was responding in a way she never expected.

"Touch me, Lauren," Italia ordered, after ripping off her tank top to expose her tanned, voluptuous breasts. Her areolas were dark and her nipples were huge from arousal. Lauren felt them tickle her own breasts. Tentatively, she obeyed and reached up to touch Italia's left nipple, feeling it in her palm and between her fingers. Italia gave out a sound of pleasure and continued to kiss Lauren, more passionately now.

Italia then wiggled out of her shorts to reveal all of her amazing naked body. Climbing back over Lauren, she reached under her nightgown to the wet area between her legs. Lauren gasped. She hadn't been touched there in ten years! Italia pushed up her nightgown to become more intimate, to kiss her where she hadn't been kissed, to tease her where she knew would bring her the most excitement. And it did.

Italia then rolled over on the bed. "Love me, Lauren. Come here and love me," she pleaded convincingly. Lauren, somewhat reluctantly, but somewhat willingly, returned the favor. She had never done anything like this before, so she just copied everything Italia did to her. Italia moaned her satisfaction, while Lauren kissed her body.

When they were content, the two of them lay naked on the bed, holding each other. They were as opposite as can be. Italia was young, tall, slender, and tan with flowing black hair; Lauren was not so young, not so tall, not so slim, and definitely white with shorter brown hair. Italia felt on top of the world; Lauren wondered how this happened. Oh, yes, it was exciting beyond belief, but she had envisioned it with Jack, as if she would be giving him her pseudo "virginity." Instead she gave "it" to Italia. She also wondered how dangerous this might be. And she asked herself, *"How jealous would Italia become if she found out about me and Jack?"* The obvious answer chilled her.

"Oh, my God, what have I done?" she screamed in her head.

❧ *B* ❧

The last thing Italia said to Lauren as she walked out the door was, "I trust you not to say anything to Jack about tonight." It felt a bit threatening. At the very least, it was a warning and it made Lauren feel uncomfortable and frightened.

Lauren closed the door and bolted it for the night. She leaned against the door for a moment, trying to compose herself. *"What the heck just happened?"* she thought. She found her half-filled wine glass and downed it.

She jumped in the shower, combed her hair, brushed her teeth, and then washed her nightgown in the sink, letting it hang dry over the shower door. In her dresser drawer she found her comfy, summer-weight, pink Hello Kitty pajamas, which she put on. She climbed into bed, but sleep evaded her. She couldn't help but think about the crazy sex she just had. Although it was exciting, Italia truly did seduce her. There was no way Italia was the childlike, delicate creature she thought she was; she was a master manipulator and intimidator! Which one was the real Italia?

She did tell Italia to stop, but it fell on deaf ears. She knew Italia wouldn't stop until she got what she wanted. She used her. She warned her not to tell Jack. Guilt laid heavily on Lauren's mind. She allowed Italia to continue, and for that she was regretful. It's strange what desire will make people do!

And what if Jack found out despite Italia's warning? She was sure it would shock him that his wife and his "sweetheart" had sex. Lauren wondered if Italia had other encounters with women in the past. It wouldn't surprise her.

The thought of the entire experience made her feel ill. Her stomach was upset and she couldn't stop trembling.

She wanted someone to talk to, but she didn't have any close personal friends. Perhaps Sue Gainer. They knew each other for years and had each other's back. Lauren decided that's what she would do first thing in the morning.

* * * * *

The sun rose early that time of year, and a ray peeked in through Lauren's curtains directly into her face. She turned and looked at the clock. 5:10 a.m. Time to get up. Her stomach was a little queasy from the night before. *"Did it really happen?"* she wondered. But then she saw the nightgown hanging in the bathroom so she knew it really did.

She chose to wear a very stylish dress with a straight skirt and a long zipper in the back. It "zipped" her up and gave her a sense of protection, as silly a notion as that was. Lauren got into the office at 7:30. Sue was already at her desk.

"Morning, Sue." she greeted.

"Morning! In early today," Sue noted.

"Um, yes. I'm wondering if I could have a word with you in the conference room."

"Now?"

"Yes, if you don't mind."

"Sure. Let's go." Thoughts raced through Sue's mind. She wondered if this was about Rennie or if she did something wrong.

Sue sat in one of the black leather chairs while Lauren, who was obviously nervous, shut the door then sat across from her.

"Sue, we've known each other a very long time. I am currently going through a personal crisis and need to have someone to talk to. If you are uncomfortable with that, let me know. I don't want to burden you," Lauren said with nervousness.

This was right up Sue's alley! There was nothing she liked better than a good mystery. She responded in a sincere voice, "I'm here for you any time you need me."

"Okay..." Lauren paused, trying to decide how to begin. "Do you know who Jack Kenner is?"

"Yes, but I never met him."

"Well, we met a few weeks ago at George's, and, long story short, we've seen each other a couple of times, but he's married."

"Oh."

"That's just the beginning of the story. I also met his wife and we've hung out several times."

"Oh!" exclaimed Sue, jumping to conclusions, although she had no idea which scenario might be the real situation.

"The problem now is that she, um, how do I put this? She wants me for herself."

"Ohhh!" Sue certainly wasn't expecting that! Her eyebrows raised but she didn't know what to say, so she said nothing and let Lauren talk.

"On top of that, my ex-husband Phil showed up and said he saw me and Jack together."

"Oh, shit!" Sue then apologized for her language, "Sorry!"

"He tried to blackmail me, but I refused."

Sue gasped.

Lauren continued, "I'm afraid he might be stalking me."

"Holy crap. Oh, sorry again."

"I don't expect you to do anything about any of this, Sue. I just want someone to know what is going on, well, in case something happens to me."

"Oh, my God!" Sue was stunned. Here was her boss in a bizarre predicament, which could lead to life-threatening situations! How things can change in an instant, all because of one decision! Sue didn't want to judge her boss; instead, she wanted to give her the benefit of the doubt. It gave Sue incentive to do more investigating, so her mind was forming a plan. "Lauren, don't worry. I promise, I'll be your eyes and ears. Let me know if anything changes."

"Thank you, Sue. Thank you," Lauren repeated with her eyes downcast in shame.

They both got up and went back to their offices without further discussion.

Lauren sighed with relief that someone knew the God's honest truth and yet would respect the secret as long as she needed to.

Sue was more determined than ever to get to the bottom of all of these mysteries. She decided that the first thing she needed to do was to get into Beeler's personnel files. This time she'd also check Jack Kenner's file.

14

"Anthony," Italia called out, as she thumbed through a magazine.

"Yeah?" He was watching a baseball game on TV, sitting in Jack's leather chair with his socked feet on the footrest.

"So, why you here anyway? You never did tell me," claimed Italia in a sisterly way.

"Eh." He put his fingers through his hair. "Got into a little trouble back home. I might have a warrant."

"A warrant? So, you bring your problems here? Don't you think they know where your sister lives?"

She wasn't thrilled with the idea of the cops coming to her home. Italia recalled, as a little girl, the police coming to their house looking for her father. Her father was angry, and unspeakable words were said as he resisted, while her mother cried and begged them not to take her husband away for the sake of the children. The police were ordering her mother not to interfere, but the situation was chaotic. Her brother called the cops "pigs," while Italia was confused and frightened by the entire scene. "Where are they taking my Papa? Why are they taking him? When will he be home again?" were her desperate questions to her mother back then, needing immediate answers. But her mother just cried and never gave a satisfactory answer, probably because she didn't know.

"I figured they wouldn't cross state lines to come look for me," Tony added.

"Does that mean you're staying for awhile?"

"Maybe."

"Who's taking care of the business?"

"I have one of the guys watching over things. It's not rocket science."

A few minutes passed, then Italia spoke up again.

"I was thinking that I'd go visit Papa and Mama this week," she proposed.

"Well, don't expect me to come. I'm happy as a clam right here." There was no way he was going back to New Jersey until things quieted down.

"Jack may not be too keen on that."

Tony was irritated. "Let Jack eat shit! It's your house, too. If it's okay with you, then he can't say nothin'."

"I suppose," she gave in. After all, she did enjoy Anthony's company while Jack was at work. As long as they were compatible and not arguing, everything was fine. Italia knew that if Anthony confronted her or started calling her derogatory names, there would be an all-out war. In that case, she would start throwing and breaking everything in her reach. It wouldn't be unusual to throw food either. The entire family did that at home while she was growing up.

She continued, "Well, I'm going to call Papa and see if this is a good week for me to visit." She went to make a call on her cell, and wandered into the kitchen. The phone rang three times before it was picked up by her mother.

"Hello," Sophia greeted in a heavy Italian accent.

"Mama, it's me, Italia."

"Oh, Italia. You no visit me in a long time. Where's your manners?" she scolded in broken English.

"I know, Mama. But I thought I'd drive up this week. How's Wednesday? It will only take me about three hours. I can be there by noon."

"Sound good. I make stuffed shells, your favorite. Come hungry."

"I will, Mama. Tell Papa I'm coming."

Her mother yelled to her husband while still on the phone, "Papa, you baby Italia's coming on Wednesday!"

"Wha? Good. It's about time! She needs to see her Papa." He walked closer to the phone with a big smile on his mustached face and grabbed the receiver from his wife's hand. "You hear that, Italia? It's about time. You bringing that no-good husband of yours, Jack?"

"No, he has to work. Papa, he's okay. You shouldn't call him names like that."

"Always working. Eh, I suppose he has to make his money to keep my *bambina* happy. Lucky for me, I got Tony taking care of business here."

"Um, right." She didn't want to admit that Tony was in Delaware and had been there for awhile. Let him get out of his own mess!

"Okay, Papa. I'll see you Wednesday! *Ciao!*"

"*Ciao, la mia dolce bambina!*"

She disconnected the call and told Anthony, "Looks like you're on your own here Wednesday and Thursday. Better plan on eating out. Jack isn't going to make dinner for you."

"Yeah, yeah. I know where McDonald's is."

* * * * *

The drive was a peaceful one. Italia thought about how her life changed when she met Lauren. She loved her. Or at least in her mind, she thought she loved her. Actually, she was totally obsessed with her. She had never made love to another woman before this. Yes, Lauren put up a little fight about it, but she succumbed to her desire. She felt the passion! It was incredible!

But Lauren was like any of the gifts Italia ever received; she loved it until it was of no more use to her. It got her excited; it made her want more, but she never considered how Lauren felt about the relationship. How could Lauren not love her body? Italia was turned on just thinking about her own body. And, oh, when she saw Lauren in that slinky nightgown, it was an invitation. She couldn't have timed it better. She played it over and over in her mind, and what she planned to do the next time. She would make it impossible for Lauren to resist her. Perhaps she would have Lauren come to her house and she could lock her in the bedroom! Italia went through the entire scenario in her mind, step by step, room by room, until they reached the bedroom. Then, anything could happen! She licked her lips in anticipation. The possibilities were endless and the thoughts were thrilling for her. She planned on setting something up when she got back home. She'd call Lauren and get the conversation started. Just hearing her voice on the other end of the phone would be exciting. Maybe Lauren was daydreaming about her, too! She hoped that was so.

Before she knew it, she arrived in Trenton at her

parents' home, a two-story, pink stucco villa with a three-car garage, a large fountain and two Roman statues, Apollo and Venus, on the well-manicured lawn. She could smell the sauce, or "gravy" as they called it, from outside the front door. She opened the door and called out, "I'm here! It smells so good, Mama!"

Her mother came from the kitchen. Italia was shocked to find her with a black eye. Her heart sunk.

"Did Papa do this to you?" she demanded to know.

Her mother just nodded and looked down in shame. Sophia wiped her hands on the full apron that she wore over her blue-flowered "housedress." Italia rarely saw her mother wear anything else besides a housedress and apron, unless they went to a wedding. It wasn't as if she couldn't afford nicer clothing; it was just part of her "role" as mother and housewife. At least the dress had some color. Over in Italy, housewives like Sophia wore black dresses every day.

"Mama, it's not your fault," Italia consoled.

"He say it is. He say the gravy is too sweet. He threw some at me," at which point she showed Italia the red burn mark on her chest.

Italia was feeling a slow burn herself, in her mind. *"Why does Papa do this?"* she thought in anger. She decided to confront him. She walked past her mother and into the living room, where her father sat in a cushy brown recliner, browsing the paper with his reading glasses low on his nose. His eyesight was worsening with age. He obviously had not heard her come in, as his hearing was not good as it used to be either.

"Papa!"

Surprised, he looked up. "Italia! Come sit by Papa." He patted the arm of the chair.

"No, Papa! Why did you hit Mama?"

He threw his paper down. "You don't need to know our business! That is between your mama and me. If she makes me angry, she gonna know it. I don't care what anyone thinks! She's my wife and she needs to do what I say!"

"Papa, you go too far! Someday you're going to regret it, that's all I'm going to say," Italia warned him.

Sophia interrupted with the words every man likes to hear, "Food's on the table." Then she added, "I hope it's 'goot.'"

Italia comforted her and said, "Of course it is, Mama. I'm sure it's *delizioso!*" Meanwhile, she glared at her father all through dinner, thinking about how she could handle this. She wasn't going to call 911; they just didn't do that in her family. Ever. If you called the police, you might not live to see tomorrow.

In addition to the stuffed shells passed around in "family style," they had fruit, bread, and antipasto, in that order. Everyone was full and Papa returned to his recliner and fell asleep. Italia and her mother cleaned up the kitchen. Sophia washed the dishes and pans in the sink, while Italia dried.

"Mama," Italia said, "why don't you leave him?" She anticipated her mother's response, hoping that she would consider it.

"And do what? Stand on the corner and beg for food?" Sophia shook her head no and put up her hands, as if she didn't want to discuss it any further.

"You can live with me. Me and Jack," Italia offered.

Italia didn't think Jack would mind. And her

mother would probably love cooking for them. Imagine eating that wonderful Italian cuisine every day!

"No, no. I belong here. Do not worry about me." Sophia didn't believe her own words, but she didn't want to make a fuss or worry Italia.

"But I do!" Italia insisted. "If you change your mind, call me. Day or night. I will come and get you."

"Okay," her mother replied but she already knew she would never call. And Italia knew it, too.

Little did Italia know that her mother had been hoarding money in her socks for the last 40 years—just in case. At last count, Sophia had amassed $395,000. *"He'll never miss a little here, a little there,"* she thought.

Italia slept there that night, but the situation weighed heavily on her mind. She worried that, someday, her father would lose control and her mother would end up in the hospital. If that happened, the hospital would notify the police, who would arrest her father on domestic violence charges. Unfortunately, he probably wouldn't have much jail time and would return home with even more anger against her mother. Knowing her mother, she would open the door and let him back in. It truly would be a vicious circle of violence.

And how would her father fare in jail? He was an old man now. He still commanded a sense of authority and the cunning to protect himself, but he no longer had the strength. It may not end well.

Anthony would have to "grow up," return to New Jersey, take care of the warrant, and look after Mama and the family business—that's all there was to it. She would have to throw him out of her house when she returned home. She just didn't know how he would react. There were times that Italia feared her brother when he got angry. Once, when they were teenagers, she saw him beat his girlfriend because she neglected to tell him where she had gone the previous night. It was just an innocent night out with her girlfriends, but Anthony couldn't reach her and that made him furious. Italia thought he was going to kill her. She knew better than to interfere. Anthony stopped short of killing the girl, thank God, but the beating left her with serious injuries. When the police investigated, the girlfriend told them she couldn't remember anything, but they suspected she was lying. They couldn't prove that Tony was involved and he got away with it. On top of all that, he discarded his girlfriend for someone new. He didn't want damaged goods. She was dead to him.

Italia and Anthony had their own run-ins, too, but Anthony knew that, if he hurt Italia, their father would unleash his own anger on him. He warned Tony never to hurt his sweet baby girl. Would he still remember that now? Italia wasn't so sure. She would have to think about how to handle him...

Italia's trip back to Delaware the next day was much more somber than the drive up. She didn't even think about Lauren.

❧ *15* ❦

Jack had customer contacts Monday morning that he could not reschedule. He took care of business as quickly as he could before returning to the office. It was imperative for him to speak with Lauren at the earliest opportunity.

At 11:15, he saw Lauren at her desk and knocked on her office partition. She looked up and smiled, but it was a nervous smile. He wondered what was wrong.

"Is everything okay?" he asked.

"Sure, Jack. How are you?" Lauren tried to speak calmly.

"Well, I would like to talk to you. Can you meet me for lunch at George's?"

Lauren paused, thinking of Phil. "Could we go somewhere else? Maybe drive separately and go to a diner?"

"We can do that. How about the Greek restaurant on 14th Street and Columbus?"

"Perfect. See you at noon." Lauren also wondered why Jack had to speak to her. Was it going to be good news or bad news?

Of course, Lauren knew that it was possible for Phil to follow either one of them to the Greek restaurant, but she was hoping she could spot him easily if she watched the door.

Jack wondered what the change in venue was all about, but it was just as well. He was thinking about Phil following them, too.

At noon, they met inside the restaurant and slid into a booth. Lauren faced the door. No sign of Phil. Jack scanned the area outside. No sign of Phil there, either.

"Thanks for meeting me," Jack said. "You look lovely." She smiled in appreciation.

The waitress came over and handed them menus. They both ordered water.

After the water glasses were on the table, Jack spoke up. "I had a visitor the other day."

She couldn't imagine who it was.

"Some guy named Phil. Your ex, perhaps?"

Lauren was truly shocked and her eyes widened. "Phil went to your house?"

"Yes. Said he'd seen us together and wanted $500."

"Oh no! You didn't give it to him, did you?"

"Well, what else could I do? Italia's brother was standing in the doorway of the house, watching and listening, but I don't think he heard your ex say he saw us together. Otherwise, he would have brought it up."

"I'm so sorry. I'll pay you back." She was truly distressed.

"No, no. I'm good for it."

The food arrived and they took a few bites. The chicken souvlaki was delicious, especially when topped with tzatziki sauce.

Jack continued, "I was taken by surprise that he knew who I was."

"I can't remember if I told you about him. He has been known to stalk me and he may have seen us at George's that first night or kissing outside on the street. Phil is very adept at finding out who people are and everything about them. He even knew about the dress I bought for the party. He had to have been following me or checking my store purchases!"

"He sounds like a creep. Is he still around? Have you seen him since?"

"No, I haven't. He only shows his face when he wants money. He has gambling debts."

"Maybe he'll leave you alone for awhile now that he has some cash. Let me know if he comes again."

"We'll figure something out...," she paused. "Meanwhile, we have to be careful," Lauren warned.

He looked at her tenderly. "We will, but that doesn't mean we can't be together." She looked up at him and wanted to kiss him, but it wasn't a private spot to do that.

He continued. "I want you to know that I've consulted a lawyer about a divorce." It was hard for him to admit, but Lauren needed to know.

"Oh, Jack, I'm so sorry. Does Italia know yet?"

"No. She'll find out soon enough."

Lauren thought about this. She didn't want to be with Italia when she got the news, that was for sure! Eventually, she or Jack would have to let Italia know about their relationship, as well. That might be even worse. She was trying not to worry about it—yet. She made a mental note to tell Sue Gainer.

Lauren asked, "Are you going to go through mediation?"

"Well, probably not. Italia will get to keep the house

and I will give her alimony. I hope that will satisfy her. I am a little worried about her mental state."

"Oh," replied Lauren nervously, thinking about what had recently transpired in her bedroom. She hoped the frightened expression on her face wasn't observed by Jack, or maybe he'd assume that her concern was about their friendship.

"Mental state?" she queried. Coming from Jack, news about Italia's mental state was very concerning to her. She needed to be more careful. *"Perhaps it would be best to keep a distance from Jack until the divorce is final,"* she thought.

"Sometimes I wonder if she isn't bi-polar or depressed. She has extreme highs and lows from day to day and it has certainly affected our relationship," he informed her. "I see it in her whole family."

"Maybe she'll get some help," she suggested.

"It's too late for us, but I hope she will find happiness. She's a beautiful woman," he stated. Lauren nodded, but wondered if his words were a little cool, after ten years of marriage. Italia still wanted to "bond" with him; he obviously was beyond that.

He turned toward her with something more on his mind. "Lauren...? Would I be able to stop by your place sometime?"

She panicked. That was the LAST thing she wanted. What if Italia saw his car parked in her driveway? Suddenly this was getting very complicated.

"You know Italia and I have been doing some 'fun things' lately." Her eyes looked downward in shame, as she recalled Italia's warning, although she was not willing to talk about it. "I'm concerned that she might see your car."

He thought about it for a moment. She was right. "There is a different place we could go. Italia doesn't know yet, but I bought a beach house and have been renovating it for the past six months. We could meet there."

"When?" She was breathless, throwing caution to the wind. Her eyes brightened and her hope grew.

"Saturday around 6 p.m.? That's when I usually go there to work. I'll e-mail you at work with the address and directions."

"I'm looking forward to it." At long last, they would be able to be alone without anyone watching or judging. And Italia knew nothing about the clandestine meeting place.

"Me, too." Then he added, "Bring a jacket. It gets cold by the water. And when you arrive, you have to park on the road, but no one will bother your car."

There was a long silence.

"Jack? Are we moving too fast?" Lauren asked poignantly.

He took her hand and sent the question back to her. "Are we? I want to get to know more about you, and I'm hoping you feel the same about me. If you decide that you don't want to pursue this relationship, I will back away. I promise you that my intentions are honest and sincere. All I know is that I want to be with you. Nothing has ever felt so right."

She nodded and squeezed his hand. "I need someone like you in my life. Right now, everything seems so crazy and out of control." He smiled and put a second hand over her hand.

But she didn't know just how crazy their relationship would get. Neither did he.

❧ 16 ❧

That afternoon Sue watched and waited for Mr. Beeler to leave his office. Luckily for her, Rennie had also stepped away from his desk. It was now or never.

She took the S-105 key out of her cup on her desk and nonchalantly strolled over to Mr. Beeler's office and opened the door, then closing it behind her. The file key worked as expected. There, in front of her, were dozens of files, each labeled with an employee's name. She grabbed Rennie's first. Setting the papers on the desk, she took an iPad photo of each one, front and back, where it went to the "cloud" so that she could also access the information from either her phone or computer. She checked the photos to make sure she could read them and they looked fairly good. Next, she pulled Jack Kenner's file and did the same thing. After she put the files back, she cleaned the door with a Kleen Wipe and closed and locked the cabinet. It had taken her five minutes. She left Beeler's office without being noticed. She sighed with relief.

Back at her desk, she opened the photos on her computer, then clicked on the first file. It was Rennie's. What she read shocked her.

"What the hell?" she whispered out loud to herself.

According to Beeler's records, Rennie was an FBI agent named Robert Sturr. Apparently, he met with Beeler once a week to brief him, without giving him specific details, but there was a name mentioned in the report—Jack Kenner! Beeler gave him the go-ahead to watch Jack's comings and goings and to have his e-mail routed through the FBI and his phone tapped.

"Holy shit!" Sue's stomach was turning. Obviously, Lauren knew nothing about this and she could very well be dragged into this.

Sue added Rennie's phone number into her contact app.

Next Sue looked at Jack's personnel file. Not much there of note. Nothing about the FBI; nothing to warrant an investigation that she could see. No crimes, no bad accounting, no complaints. Not even a bad review! She also put his address and phone number into her contact file, as well as his "next of kin" and family members. It listed his father, John Kenner (deceased), mother Helen Kenner, and wife Italia Marconi Kenner. Oddly, it also listed Italia's family as well, including her father Dominic Marconi, mother Sophia Marconi, and brother Anthony Marconi, all of Trenton.

Since Sue wasn't sure why they were watching him, she didn't want to get into more trouble by tipping off Lauren or Jack. She was already in trouble by copying the files. And she had tailed an FBI agent recently. *"Crap."* she thought. *"I hope I didn't drag myself into this! Now Rennie, er, Robert, may be watching **me**!"*

She went in to see Lauren, who seemed more

relaxed now. "Hi. How's it going?" Sue asked.

"Better, thanks. Jack and I had lunch today and he's aware of my ex. So that cat is out of the bag!"

"Nice. You guys doing anything special?"

Lauren whispered, "Going to his beach house this weekend! Don't tell anyone!" She was beaming.

"Wow, good for you," Sue replied, all the while getting a bad vibe. This was not good, but she couldn't stop her.

Sue wondered what to do. She decided to forget Rennie for now and focus on Jack. She needed to understand why the FBI would be interested in him. She went back to her computer and researched Jack. Strangely, records didn't list him as the owner of his current address. Public tax records were in the name of Italia Marconi Kenner! *"So, his wife owns the house and not Jack! Wow!"* Sue thought in amazement. Next she Googled Dominic Marconi. There were several articles on his arrests, convictions, and brief prison time in his younger years. Then she Googled Anthony Marconi. There were newspaper articles about him, too—aggravated assault with a deadly weapon, resisting arrest, and solicitation. *"Oh my God. No wonder the FBI is looking at Jack's e-mail and listening in on his phone! It's the family, or should I say, her family!"* She hoped that Jack was not involved in any of that shady business. Lauren didn't need any more drama.

After work, she drove to Jack's neighborhood—beautiful homes on a winding suburban road. There was a wooded area where she parked without raising the suspicion of the neighbors and where she could see Jack's driveway. Sue sat there and watched until the sun went down. She saw lights go on in a couple of rooms. No one left the residence by 10 p.m., so she decided to resume the watch the next few nights. She had no proof that anything would happen at all, and it might not even happen here. She'd just have to keep her eyes and ears open, as she promised Lauren.

It was Saturday afternoon when FBI Agent Robert Sturr stopped in to see Lieutenant Fitch. They shook hands and Agent Sturr sat in his padded guest chair.

Mike informed him of the latest lab results. "Agent Sturr, we have something for you. The bullet you brought in to us from the gun range matched the bullet found at the crime scene."

"I knew it!" blurted out Agent Sturr with a grin. "We got him."

"We'll have a search warrant signed by the judge, and we'll have our Gang Unit serve it. And we'll engage a K-9 unit because of the severity of the crime. Depending on what we find, you can serve the arrest warrant whenever you're ready."

"Perfect. I want to be there at the house today."

"Sure. Just let our guys do their thing first."

"Got it."

* * * *

Jack left the house at the same time he did every Saturday night. Italia never asked any questions. Tonight, she was with her brother, at least, so she wasn't as lonely.

"Hey, Sis. Get me a beer." Tony sat stretched out in Jack's recliner, pushing the remote buttons for the large-screen TV.

Italia went to the refrigerator then returned to the family room where she handed him the beer. "Here ya go, Anthony." He downed a few gulps, then placed the bottle on a side table.

She thought about going over to see Lauren again, but she hadn't heard from her. She thought she'd at least text or call after their encounter, but there was no communication. That concerned Italia a little, but she hadn't called her either. Maybe she was just busy, or waiting for her to make the next move. Yes, that had to be it.

Italia thought about the sex. It was very exciting to think about. She found herself staring into space and reliving every delicious moment over and over. She felt her nipples getting hard and a desire in her groin. She slipped upstairs, dropped her clothing to the floor, and got into her bed to masturbate. She was in the middle of a climax when she heard pounding on the front door and a shouting voice that said, "Police! Search warrant! Come out now with your hands up! We have a dog and he will bite!" It heightened her climax and she reached it and moaned loudly. She heard the same voice shouting again, "Police! Come out now! We have a dog and he will bite!" This time it broke her concentration.

"Anthony," she yelled downstairs, "For God's sake, go to the door. It's the police!" She put her fingers back in her vagina where she was still sensitive and tried for a second climax.

Tony knew well enough who was at the door. He

had been through this a number of times. He yelled back, "I'm coming out. Hold your fire." He didn't think he had anything to worry about.

As he opened the front door, the police shouted, "Hold your hands above your head where we can see them!" He did as he was told.

"We have a search warrant," the police informed Tony. "We need you to step outside. Keep your hands up," they ordered.

Two officers in protective gear and armed with AK-47s pointed their guns at him, while two others cuffed him.

"What's your name?" they demanded to know.

"Anthony Marconi."

"You are being detained. Who else is in the house?"

"My sister, Italia. She's upstairs. She might be sleeping."

"Who else?"

"No one."

They needed to find the home owner and present her with the warrant. Other officers established a perimeter around the house to ensure that no one left the premises from the patio door.

A line of police officers cleared the downstairs and headed upstairs. As they swung the door open to Italia's bedroom, they found her naked in bed with her fingers inside herself and in the middle of her second climax. "Ah, ah, AHHH!" she screamed. The police were speechless for a moment, then told her to get her clothes on. As she slipped on her shorts and top, she made sure she put on a show for them, exposing her bare butt and bending over to put on her shorts. She asked, "What's going on?" At the same time, she thought, *"Damn! They ruined a good climax!"*

"We'll explain everything to you once you are outside. Right now, you are detained." They put her in handcuffs. "Is there anyone else in the house?"

"No. Hey, these cuffs hurt! Can't you loosen them? I haven't done anything!" She whipped her hair around so that it hit the officer in the face.

"Where is Jack Kenner?"

"I don't know. He's not home."

They escorted her down the stairs and out of the house, and then explained that they had a search warrant. They allowed Italia and Tony to sit on the bumper of Tony's Range Rover. Much to Tony's relief, they did not have a search warrant for his vehicle, nor did they have a warrant for his arrest. Or, at least, they hadn't mentioned it yet. It was possible that they didn't know about the warrant out of New Jersey. That didn't mean that one of the officers wouldn't check his record while the others searched the house. He certainly wasn't going to bring it up.

The police were at the house for a couple of hours, tearing everything apart and looking in every "nook and cranny." They came out with Jack's gun case, a box containing his computer, and evidence bags, one containing the empty Corona bottle that had been sitting next to the recliner, and another bag packed with dark clothing. Agent Sturr was there to observe firsthand. He didn't miss a thing.

Tony maintained a deadpan face. He knew this could go two ways: either they were interested in Jack for whatever reason, or they would discover his warrant. He took dibs on Jack, and kept his mouth shut. Perhaps it had something to do with the dude in the driveway the other day. Maybe Jack was dealing. Maybe the guy was an undercover cop! Wouldn't that be funny? Tony chuckled to himself. He secretly hoped that was it.

Italia was irritated about the search. She hoped they wouldn't confiscate her money. They didn't; it was all still there when she checked later.

Once the police left, Tony and Italia went back in the house. Tony was relieved that he hadn't been arrested. The house was a mess so Italia started to pick things up, and was pissed that Jack was not home to handle this. She wondered why they were looking for him and what he had done. Perhaps it had something to do with where he went every Saturday night. He never got home till way after midnight. She decided it was time to find out what he was up to. Was he involved in something illegal? Was he with some other woman? It was hard to imagine that he was into dealing drugs, as he was so straight laced. That didn't mean his activities were not criminal. Maybe he was embezzling from his company. That was believable. What if he were a killer? That thought unsettled her a bit. Sometimes you just never knew. Her suspicious mind was not satisfied. She'd have it out with him as soon as he got home. She momentarily felt a little fear. She didn't want to rouse a sleeping bear, so to speak. She thought about the anger in her own father and brother once again.

You just never knew who could turn out to be a killer. Anyone was capable.

* * * * *

Agent Sturr, aka Rennie, was disappointed that they had missed Jack, but it wasn't a lost night. He got his eyes on Tony and he was familiar with his arrest record. And he had heard about how Mrs. Kenner was found naked in her bed. He tried to imagine it and was sorry he missed it. "Damn," he said out loud, as he got behind the wheel of his car. Nevertheless, it made him grin. She was hot stuff!

There was one more lead to follow. In Jack's e-mail at work, he sent Lauren an address at the beach. He was on his way there now.

$$\approx 18 \approx$$

t 5 p.m. Sue was sitting in her car, spying on Jack's house, when a police SWAT team vehicle flew by, followed by a few police cars. Shocked at their appearance, Sue pulled down the brim of her red cap and ducked to let them pass. Then she peeked to see what was going on. It was like a scene from a TV show. They exited their tank-like vehicle at Jack's house and ran up to the door, with three officers at the door and two other officers dispersing in two directions to surround the house. They were dressed in their bulletproof vests, carrying AK-47s, and leading one K-9 officer. She saw the lead officer use his fist to pound on the door and yell to the occupants to come out. Guns were pointed at the door, as it slowly opened. A stocky, dark-haired man stepped out, with his hands up. He was wearing a black t-shirt and jeans and no shoes.

The man who came out was put in cuffs. He didn't resist. She wasn't certain, but he may have been Jack's brother-in-law, Anthony Marconi, whose name was listed in the Personnel file. Then the police entered the residence, each officer holding the shoulder of the officer in front of him. A few minutes passed before a slim woman in short shorts was guided outside by the arm by one of the SWAT team members, and she was also in cuffs. Sue knew she had to be Jack's wife. Apparently, Jack wasn't there, as they didn't bring anyone else out of the house.

Sue thought about what Lauren had mentioned in the office, that she and Jack had plans to go to their secret rendezvous—the beach house. She didn't know where it was, but she had to assume that Jack had already gone there and Lauren had met him there.

She watched as the police completed their search, removing "evidence," and loading it into a vehicle.

After about two hours, things seemed to be wrapping up and Sue observed that both residents had their cuffs removed. They rubbed their wrists and waited for the police to leave before going back into the house. Eventually, she saw Rennie get into his Crown Vic, leaving the scene. After he passed her parked Corolla without so much as a glance, she turned her car around and followed him, giving him much a bigger lead than the last time and putting several cars between them. She suspected that he was probably onto her, but she followed anyway. He didn't try to ditch her this time.

Sue thought, *"If I play detective again, I'm going to have to buy a car that isn't brilliant blue."*

They got onto Route 1 and followed it along the ocean. Rennie started to slow down, she assumed to look at house numbers. The long, summer days allowed plenty of light to read the lettering on mailboxes, even at 8 p.m. She saw him pull over to the side of the road. She stopped as far back as she could without losing sight of him. He didn't get out of his car right away, so she waited in hers, too, until he exited his vehicle and headed for the door. At that point, she moved her car closer and waited. She was extremely tense as she sat there, wondering what was going on inside the house. Then she saw a movement in the bushes... *"What is that?"*

* * * * *

Just before 6 p.m., Lauren parked her car on the road, grabbed her purse and zippered sweatshirt, and walked to the cute gray bungalow with white shutters. She knocked on the door. Jack's smiling face greeted her as he ushered her inside. After closing the door, the first thing he did was put his arms around her and kiss her. She immediately relaxed in his arms, dropping her purse and sweatshirt on the floor and returning the kiss. It was a long, warm embrace. She also felt relief. Alone with Jack, at last.

"Would you like to see what I've done with the place?" he asked with pride.

Jack showed her around, noting the work that he had done himself and what still needed to be done. The plumbing and electrical were finished and the inspections completed. The bathroom fixtures were installed as well as the mirror, light, and fan. It was the only room finished. The rest of the ceilings were in place, with holes cut out for lighting fixtures. He hung some temporary LED lights so he could see what he was doing during those late nights. The next step was to insulate the walls and add drywall to the rest of the house. After the drywall finishing and two coats of paint, he still had to put in kitchen cabinets, lighting, countertops, flooring, and moldings. A lot of work on Saturday nights, but worth the effort.

"You're doing an amazing job!" Lauren congratulated. "It's going to be gorgeous!" She looked out the windows to the ocean.

"I do have some food in a mini fridge and a microwave to heat things up, if you're hungry."

"Not right now, thanks," she declined.

"Would you like to take a walk?" Jack offered.

"I'd love to." Their eyes met and Jack took her in his arms for another long kiss.

"I'm so glad you're here," he said, smiling.

"Me, too." Lauren's stomach was doing somersaults and she was trembling a little from the excitement of being with Jack.

"Ready? Be careful on the steps." He opened the door for her and took her hand as she descended three wooden steps to a sandy yard. She put on her sweatshirt.

As Jack and Lauren took a long walk on the sand, holding hands, he reminded Lauren that he had spoken with a divorce lawyer. Lauren asked, "Are you sure you want to go forward with that?"

"I don't see another alternative. You and I could still see each other secretly, but how long would that last? Italia will find out sooner or later. And it's just not about us. I've been contemplating this for awhile—before I even met you. We just aren't happy anymore."

Lauren's eyes were downcast as she thought about the sex she had with Italia. She didn't have the nerve to tell Jack. In fact, she wanted to forget the whole scenario. *Where was my mind when I gave in to Italia?"* she questioned herself. She felt like a coward. Other times, she felt that she was pressured by Italia. And, if she told Jack, would he forgive her? She was worried that he might not. He might be shocked and even disgusted.

She decided not to mention anything to Jack, unless it came out at a later date. She would deal with it then.

They walked along the shoreline, carrying their sandals, where the tide was slowing coming in. She studied his face as they chatted. He had perfect lips, a fine nose, high forehead, blue eyes, and long eyelashes. So far, he had a good head of hair. It was starting to turn gray, but it looked good on him. Today, the ocean breeze blew a lock of his hair onto his forehead, making him appear younger.

When they were out of sight of all the beach houses, they stopped to kiss, with the cool surf reaching their bare feet in gentle waves. They stood in a tender embrace, exchanging "butterfly" kisses, as their lips lightly touched, prompting more and more kisses—deeper kisses, as they explored each other's mouths. He put his fingers through her hair, continued to kiss her sweet lips, then her cheeks and forehead, whispering words of endearment and love. "Lauren, how I've waited for this moment!" he murmured between kisses. "I need you so much. I want you so much," he begged, as he pulled her closer to his body, if that was possible. He fantasized about making love to her and satisfying the burning desire that he felt.

For Lauren, it ignited a passion she had not experienced in many years. Her arms went around his body, feeling his muscular shoulders as he held her. When he pulled her closer, she "lost herself" in his embrace. She felt desirable, even "hot," forgetting all the doubts about herself and whether or not she could fall in love again. Most importantly, she felt loved—after all the misery with Phil and all the years without affection. Here was the man she dreamed about for weeks, kissing her on a beach and saying that he needed her! Those words filled her heart with joy! She responded to his passion with her own yearnings. "Jack, I need you, too. You're all I can think about. You're all I want." He kissed her harder on the lips, sealing their new-found love for each other.

Their kisses became more ardent and they collapsed into the warm sand, wrapping themselves in a passionate embrace, and letting their hands explore each other's body as they smothered each other with more kisses. He put his hand under her sweatshirt and top and felt her firm breasts and aroused nipples. Lauren responded to his tease with a gasp and gentle moaning. She wanted his touch to be even more intimate. She reached for his shorts and felt his erection. He whispered in her ear, "Mmm... That feels so good."

After they caressed each other for awhile, Jack looked in her gentle, brown eyes and longingly said, "Let's go back to the house. I want to make love to you. If that's okay with you." He knew she was ready but he let her make the choice.

Although she hated to stop their playful exploration, Lauren nodded in agreement. "I want to make love to you, too," she admitted.

The thought of being next to Jack's naked body excited her tremendously. And she wanted his hands all over her body, discovering all the things that thrilled her. Jack helped her to her feet and they put their arms around each other's waist as they walked back to his house and beckoning bed.

In the house, he ushered Lauren into the bedroom that overlooked the ocean. The view was spectacular without window coverings and they could watch the waves rolling in on the beach, if that's what they wanted to do. Just not tonight. Despite the bedroom's rough construction, there was a queen-sized feather bed with clean linens, two pillows, and a light aqua coverlet. What else did they need?

He drew Lauren close and kissed her lips, which were open slightly as an invitation. It didn't take long for their bodies to heat up and respond. Jack removed her top, revealing two perfect, round "peaches" that he kissed lovingly. They removed the rest of their clothing and embraced, naked. The feel of his skin on hers took her breath away. Jack's reaction was slightly different, as he already had an erection. He looked at her body and told her she was beautiful. She responded with a deep kiss. Then he cupped her left breast with his right hand and teased her nipple. Her eyes closed in excitement and she felt fire in her groin. She reached for his privates and massaged and squeezed them. Jack gasped this time, feeling her soft hands on his hot and hard body parts. He again kissed her lips, letting his passion take over and their tongues go deep. He put his hand between her legs and found her wet and ready. When he touched her there, her body shook with pleasure. She needed him—now!

They collapsed on the old iron bed, which creaked with every move. They continued to passionately kiss as their hands touched every part of their eager bodies. He lightly bit her nipples, bringing her more delight, then pushed himself up to her soft lips. They were body to body, lips to lips.

Jack softly asked, "Do you want me, Lauren? All of me?"

There was no question. She begged, "Please! I want to be one with you." She had been waiting for this for weeks; she didn't want to wait a minute more. She gave herself freely to him.

She tried to make the ecstasy last as long as possible, but the wave of excitement washed over her and she climaxed, crying out with unbelievable satisfaction and joy. She was his, and he was hers. She cried, "Oh my God, Jack, you feel incredible! Please don't stop!" She was still sensitive so he continued until she came again. She had never felt such release! There was nothing to separate them.

Jack increased his pace, feeling the momentum build to a frenzy, until he came with a long, loud cry. They both expressed their "Oh, my Gods" over and over, as they kissed and their sweaty bodies rested against each other. As he started to relax after his climax, Jack gushed, "Oh! Thank you, baby. That was wonderful!" He kissed her hair and her face, with sweat coming from his brow. He couldn't get enough of her. They both giggled with their new-found joy.

It was magical, mystical, unforgettable, and worth all the risks. Nothing else mattered. Time didn't even exist. They belonged to each other. They were now committed to each other. Their lives would never be the same.

After they rested in each other's arms, they knew they eventually had to get up and dressed. It was difficult to part, but they were both sure that this relationship would not end with this one intimate encounter. But they understood that they needed to get beyond some serious hurdles in order to solidify their relationship and be together permanently. They were willing to work at it, no matter what it took or what happened.

As Lauren was cleaning up, putting on her clothes, and brushing her hair while looking in the bathroom mirror, Jack took it all in. Here was a mature woman with a kind heart. No complaints about her own body, her clothes, her surroundings, like "someone" he knew. And she was very attractive. He had to admit that he thoroughly enjoyed fantasizing about her before their encounter today. In fact, he knew he would be doing a lot more fantasizing now.

When they both looked presentable, Lauren gave him a tender goodbye kiss near the door.

"Jack, I'm so glad we finally got together."

"Me, too. I can't describe how I feel about you."

"I feel the same way," she said as she snuggled into his shoulder. "I don't want to leave!" But it was getting dark and she had a fairly long ride home.

Suddenly, there was a loud knock on the door, which startled both of them. Jack broke the embrace, while Lauren straightened her clothes and hair. Jack opened the door to see a familiar face: Rennie.

Lauren couldn't understand why Rennie, of all people, would be at Jack's beach house. Jack was confused as well. He had seen Rennie at work, but he didn't know him.

"Jack Kenner?" Rennie asked.

"Yes. What do you want?"

Rennie showed him his FBI credentials. "I'm Agent

Sturr with the FBI."

"What?" Jack and Lauren exclaimed at the same time. They couldn't believe their ears. "Is this a joke?" added Jack.

"Jack Kenner, you're being detained. No joke." Rennie got out his cuffs and asked Jack to put his hands behind his back. "Do you have anything on you that will stick me or poke me?"

"No," Jack replied. "What's this all about?"

"Do you have any weapons in the house or on you?"

"No!"

After Rennie cuffed him and patted him down, he sat Jack down and came over to Lauren. "You're being detained, too, temporarily. Do you have any weapons on you?"

"No!" She looked at Jack, pleadingly. He shook his head, confused. She was trembling. Just a few minutes before, they were in heaven. Now they were in hell.

"This is just for my safety, Ms. Miller, until a backup unit comes. I need Jack to come to police headquarters for questioning."

"Questioning? About what?" Jack asked incredulously. Agent Sturr did not reply. Instead, he just had them sit on the bed while he made a call on his cell.

"Yeah. This is FBI Agent Sturr. I need a transport..." He gave them the address.

After Agent Sturr hung up, Jack angrily blurted out, "I know my rights! You need to tell me what this is all about. Why do you need to question me? I don't know anything about any crime!"

"Relax, Jack. You're not under arrest. You're being detained."

"Why does Lauren have to be handcuffed? You don't need her."

"It'll just be a few more minutes. I'm sorry, but I have to follow protocol. Just relax."

Soon the police car arrived to pick up Jack. Lauren, feeling very confused and frightened, was eventually released from the handcuffs, as she watched her lover being taken away.

During all of this, there was someone standing outside, out of sight of the traffic on the road, peeking in a side window and watching everything that was going down.

19

At headquarters, Jack was put in Room 2, a cold, stark room with an uncomfortable metal chair, where he waited for quite some time. The door opened and two police detectives entered. One detective removed his cuffs and then both sat across from him. Agent Sturr sat in a nearby room watching the monitor as the session was recorded.

"Hi, Jack. My name is Lt. Mike Fitch, Major Crimes, and this is Detective Al White. Do you know why you're here today?"

"I have no idea!" Jack responded with fear in his voice. But he thought it was interesting that Detective White was actually black.

The seasoned detectives were masters of interrogation. They knew that they'd get more information when they were respectful, made "friends" with the "persons of interest," and spoke their language. With Jack, they didn't need to use street talk. He was a well-educated, sensible person from a good environment. But they did need to get the truth out of him.

"Jack, as you may know, we, in Major Crimes, investigate homicides," explained Lt. Fitch.

Jack waited, confused.

"Can you tell us where you were on Sunday, July 16, at approximately 2 a.m.?" Fitch asked.

Jack thought for a moment. "Well, every Saturday night I go to my beach house where I was detained tonight. So, about that time I was on my way home."

"Did you stop anywhere?"

"No. That's late. I've been doing renovation work and I'm tired by midnight or 1 a.m. I just want to get home to bed."

"Were you alone?"

"Yes."

Lt. Fitch wrote down some notes. "Did you stop for a drink, Jack?"

"No."

"Have you ever been to Roscoe's Fox Den?"

Jack had heard of it, and knew it was a shady establishment.

"Never."

Lt. Fitch leaned forward on the table and looked him in the eye. "Jack, what if I told you that someone saw you there."

Jack's eyes opened wide. "That's a downright lie! I've never been there, I tell you! Who told you that?" he demanded to know. Neither detective reacted nor responded.

"Did you have your gun with you that night?"

"No!" Jack pounded his fist on the table. "I have a Concealed Carry permit, but I rarely ever carry." Jack was getting livid with the accusations and lies.

"Okay, Jack. Relax. We're just looking for the truth here. Just tell us the truth and we can make this go quicker."

"I AM telling the truth!" he blurted out. Then Jack

sat back in his chair, frustrated and tired of all this. He couldn't understand why he was here or why he was put in handcuffs to begin with! And who said they saw him at that seedy bar? Where was this going? Were they going to put him in jail?

Fitch changed the line of questioning. "Jack, tell us what you know about your brother-in-law."

Jack calmed down. "Tony? Well, I don't care for him but my wife is fond of him. I think he's kind of a bully."

"Is he living with you?"

"No, but he has been staying with us for a few weeks. He works for his father. He must be on vacation."

"What kind of business does your father-in-law have, Jack?"

"Amusement games. They lease bowling machines, pinball machines, and jukeboxes to bars. That sort of thing. Tony's a salesman and an accountant, my wife tells me. I never talk to him about his job. I try not to ever talk to him—period!"

"An accountant, huh?" Both detectives looked at each other and quietly snickered. "Are you aware of his arrest record, Jack?"

"Arrest record? Well, I know he's been in bar fights. He has a big mouth. Doesn't know when to shut up and he doesn't take shit from anybody. I try not to get in his way."

"Does he have a gun with him?" the detective queried.

"He may have. I'm not sure. I haven't seen one."

"Tell us about your gun, Jack," Detective White asked.

Riled up, Jack thought, *"Here we go again!"* He replied, "It's a Smith & Wesson 9mm 15 plus 1. You guys probably knew that already."

"When was the last time you used it?"

"At the shooting range on Oceanside a week ago."

"Does anyone else ever use your gun?"

"My wife used it at the gun range the same day."

"How about Tony? Has he ever used it?"

"No. Not to my knowledge. I keep it in a case in my office desk." Jack paused. "Wait a minute! I noticed that my gun case wasn't in the same spot when I took it to the range! I don't know if Italia moved it or if Tony did. He certainly had access to it."

"Where was Tony on the night of July 15th and the morning of the 16th?" Lt. Fitch asked.

"I don't know about the 15th. I came home around 3 a.m. on the 16th and he was in the living room talking to Italia."

"What was he wearing?"

"Black jeans and a black t-shirt, black shoes. There was a black jacket on a chair."

"What did he say to you?"

"Nothing. Not even hello. Italia told me he came to the house before midnight, then went out for beer, then came back to the house just before I got home, like I said, about 3 a.m. He was going to stay with us for a couple of weeks, which I wasn't happy about."

"What kind of beer does he drink?"

"Corona."

The detectives looked at each other.

"Okay, Jack. Just stay put for a little while. We'll be back." Fitch and Detective White got up and left the room, locking it behind them. Fitch turned to White,

“Keep him on ice for now.”

Jack sighed and put his head down. He thought about Lauren and hoped she was okay. He hoped he would be okay, too!

❧ 20 ❧

It was 9 a.m. on Sunday morning and Jack still wasn't home. As Italia checked the clock, she was pissed. First, the police raided their house the day before and took their computer, their gun, and various other things, and then Jack didn't even have the courtesy to call to say he was not coming home. How dare he! She wondered if he spent the night with another woman. Is that where he had been going every Saturday night? And she trusted him! That thought really made her angry. Never once did she consider that her rendezvous with Lauren was cheating or how Jack would react or feel about that. To Italia, it wasn't cheating because she was with another woman—a friend, not a male love interest.

Tony got up and was walking around in his plaid boxer shorts. Irritated, Italia commented, "Can't you put some clothes on?"

"Those damn cops took one of my shirts and jeans. Does Jack have anything I can wear?"

"Go ahead and look. I'm so pissed at him for not coming home, I'm ready to throw his clothes out on the lawn!" Tony went back upstairs to look in Jack's closet.

The doorbell rang. She thought it might be Jack if

he lost his keys. She opened the door, ready to chastise him, and saw a middle-aged man standing there. He was dressed in wrinkled beige pants and a yellow short-sleeved, button-down shirt, and he was holding a large manila envelope. An old Buick was parked in the driveway.

"Yes?"

"Mrs. Kenner? I have something you might be interested in. Can I come in?" He gave her the once-over, focusing on her breasts.

She caught him looking at her chest and snarled, "I don't think so. What do you want?"

"I'm Phil, Lauren's ex-husband. Can I talk to you?"

Her suspicious demeanor changed to one of concern. "Oh! Is she okay?" Several thoughts went through her mind. Perhaps she was sick and this "Phil" was letting her know. Or maybe she was in the hospital!

"I'm sure she's fine. I have some pictures you might be interested in."

Italia breathed a sigh of relief. "Come in," she said politely. Italia showed him to the kitchen and they stood by the island where they had good light. She didn't know what to expect. Just maybe she'd see pictures of Lauren naked, but why would her ex have them? She anxiously awaited the viewing, with her eyes fixed on the envelope, as Phil untwisted the tie. He was watching her and recognized the anticipation in her eyes. He wondered what she knew or didn't know, but she was going to find out. Real fast. He was enjoying this.

He opened the manila envelope, pulled out the contents, and displayed twelve pictures of her husband and Lauren making love in various poses and positions in some strange, unfinished house.

"What the fuck is this?" She turned her anger toward Phil, as she grabbed one of the photos of Lauren and Jack, naked, in bed.

"Let's just say it's an insurance policy. $10,000 and they are yours," he offered. "I know you're good for it...with a family like yours." He looked directly into her black eyes with no emotion. Just a cold, hard stare.

She glared at him. "How dare you!" she growled.

"I can take them back, but then you won't have much proof for divorce court."

Italia wanted to weep. There, in the pictures, were the two people she loved most, trusted most. Betraying her!!

She thought about what he said for a long moment. She wanted those pictures! Not necessarily for divorce court. More for revenge. "Fine. But if you ever come back for more money, I will kill you." She meant it. She would have shot him today if the police hadn't taken Jack's gun.

She went to where she hid a private stash of money, leaving Phil alone in the kitchen. Luckily, the police did not confiscate it. She counted out $10,000. She knew she could get more from her father if she needed it. That's all she had to do was ask. He'd do anything for his sweet baby girl. But for now, she had enough to pay for the wretched pictures in Phil's possession. She sobbed and seethed at the same time.

Phil saw the money in her shaking hand and wondered if he shouldn't have made the price higher. Maybe next time. And there would be a next time. He was already planning his next move. This cash would tide him over for a little while. He could have a little fun until it ran out or until some "wiseguy" found out about it. He would have to hide it somewhere safe.

"Remember what I said. If you ask for more money, I will kill you," Italia warned in the most serious voice.

Phil wasn't put off by Italia nor did he feel worried or threatened. He was just interested in the cash in his palm. It was so easy! A sure bet! *"Well, Lauren, you should have given me the $500,"* he thought to himself. *"You're gonna be sorry now. Never underestimate me again, Sweetheart, and don't piss me off!"*

"Right, right. I thank you very much for your business, Mrs. Kenner. Enjoy your photos." He laughed as he walked out to his car. He cranked the key and a puff of black smoke came out of the tail pipe.

Italia watched him drive away then went back to the envelope sitting on the kitchen island. She spread out the photos and examined them one by one. Normally, she would have been turned on by the naked pictures of Lauren—and, yes, Jack. But not today. Today she was angry. Today she was full of rage. Today she wanted revenge. Today she wanted them dead!

21

S ue Gainer was the only person to see the strange guy creeping around the beach house where she had followed Rennie that Saturday night. At first, it appeared that he was looking in the windows, but then Sue realized he had a camera and was taking pictures. It occurred to her that this could be Lauren's stalker—her ex-husband! That could only mean one thing—selling pictures for a price. She figured that he was going to blackmail either Jack or his wife, and the wife made more sense.

Rennie had been inside the beach house for at least twenty minutes. Then, to her shock, a police cruiser arrived and took Jack away in handcuffs! "What the fuck!" she exclaimed out loud. She wondered if he really was involved in some shady deal. Lauren must have been left behind since she was not taken in a police car. But the guy who was peering in the windows slipped away, got into an old Buick, and drove off before the police or Rennie caught sight of him. Sue decided to follow him. She hated to leave Lauren by herself, but Sue had no reason to be there, Lauren appeared to be safe, and she needed to see what this guy was going to do next.

He drove all the way back from the beach into town

and pulled into the parking lot of a drug store with late hours. Sue waited until he returned to his car carrying a familiar envelope with photographic prints—perhaps 8x10s, which he probably made himself at a kiosk.

It was getting late, and Sue decided to resume her watch on Sunday. She also needed a potty break and something to eat, and her pets Henry and Butterscotch needed food and water, too.

Early the next morning Sue parked again in the wooded area by Jack's house to see what might happen next.

She didn't have to wait long. The same Buick from the night before pulled into Jack's driveway, then the "ex" got out, holding a manila envelope. He rang the doorbell and Jack's wife came to the door, wearing pink short shorts and a white halter top. After about ten minutes, he went back out to his car in the driveway empty handed. He had a big smirk on his face. "Asshole," Sue said aloud. She watched him drive by her car.

Sue wasn't quite sure what to do next. Lauren was probably home and, no doubt, distraught. Jack was with the police. Rennie, aka Agent Sturr, followed the police cruiser last night and she didn't tail them. Jack's wife was in the house, probably in shock. She sat there for several minutes sorting things out. Suddenly, the door to Jack's garage opened and a black Range Rover backed out. When the vehicle passed her, she noticed there was a dark-haired man behind the wheel. The rest of the windows were darkly tinted. *"Boyfriend? Brother?"* Sue wondered. She decided it must be Jack's brother-in-law because, even with a quick glance, she saw that it was the same man who was detained during the raid. She was going to find out where he was going and what he was going to do.

The guy, whom Sue started calling "BIL" for brother-in-law, drove into a run-down area of the city where he went up to the door of a two-story green house with a rickety porch. Sue stuck out like a sore thumb in her bright blue Corolla but she parked a half-block away and locked her doors. Sue was nervous seeing a few men in hoodies (in mid-summer!) gathering on the corner, but no one bothered her. BIL was in and out in about four minutes. *"Enough to buy drugs,"* she figured at first, but then her next thought was *"or a gun."* That concerned her. She gave him a head start, then started to follow him again. "Where is he going to go next?" Sue said aloud to herself.

The black Range Rover got on the expressway, as Sue tailed several cars back. The Range Rover exited in a much nicer residential area, going faster than the speed limit, and she tried not to lose sight of him as he made a few turns. When he pulled into a housing tract, she didn't want to be noticed, so she slowed down. As she got closer to his destination, she saw the street sign—Sandstone Lane—that sounded very familiar. "Sandstone, Sandstone," she repeated. Then it dawned on her—he was going to Lauren's house!! This could not be good.

She pulled over to the edge of the road. Her heart was beating rapidly. Her mind raced. *"What the hell am I going to do? I don't have any proof of a crime to call 911. I don't have a gun. Oh, my God! What am I going to do? The hell of a detective I am!"*

Sue saw the SUV pull into a driveway ahead. BIL got out of the driver's seat and Jack's wife got out of the back seat! She must have been there all the time and the tint must have hidden her from view! The two of them looked like they were on a mission as they went up to the front door.

Sue started to panic.

Suddenly, she thought about Rennie. Sue remembered that she had his personnel file on her iPad and his cell phone number in her contact list! It seemingly took forever to find the information, but she finally located it and dialed his number on her cell phone. "Answer, you son of a bitch! Answer!" she yelled to no one.

$$\circ\!\!\!\circ \ \ 22 \ \ \circ\!\!\!\circ$$

Lauren was still distraught the day after her rendezvous with Jack and the subsequent arrival of Agent Sturr who whisked Jack away. It was a stressful drive home. She didn't even know how she got there! All she could think about was Jack. She hadn't slept a wink and had been crying almost all night. She paced the floor and rubbed her forehead and face out of worry. Why hadn't Jack called? Where was he? Was he okay? Why did the police have to question him? She thought about calling the police, but what good would that do? She just had to wait...

The doorbell rang. She wiped her eyes and blew her nose before going to the door. She prayed that it wasn't Italia looking for another encounter. She also prayed that it was Jack, free from police interrogation. The person she saw standing there confused her. It was Italia's brother. Then she saw Italia standing behind him, holding a large envelope. They did not look friendly. A chill went down her spine.

She started to say, "This isn't a good time," but she barely got out two words when they forced themselves inside, closed the door and bolted it, which set off silent alarm bells in Lauren's head. Tony took Lauren by the arm and forced her into the kitchen.

Then Tony drew a gun from the back of his pants. Lauren had no idea what kind it was, but what did that matter? Every gun can kill. She stared down the barrel in fear.

"What's going on?" she cried. There were four negative scenarios that she imagined: 1. Jack had been arrested for some terrible crime and they thought she was involved. 2. The police told Italia about finding her and Jack at the beach home. 3. Jack came home, admitted their affair, and begged forgiveness. 4. Jack was dead. There may have been other scenarios, but she didn't have time to think logically. All of them struck terror in her heart.

Lauren started to back up.

"Don't move or I'll kill you right now!" Tony ordered with a voice like cold steel.

Lauren stopped and took a quick breath in.

Italia, who was purple with rage, started whipping the large envelope in her face. "You bitch! You betrayed me! You made love to me then stole my husband?" Tony's eyes darted toward Italia with her admission of a same-sex romantic encounter. Did he just hear her right? He was speechless for the first time in many years.

Italia continued, "How long has this been going on? How dare you? You made a fool of me! You shamed me and my family! Do you know who I am? Do you know what we can do to you?"

In response, Lauren shook her head. She knew she was in grave danger. This wasn't the fragile Italia she once knew, or even Italia, the hot and sexy lover. This was the wild-with-anger Italia. Dangerous Italia with her evil brother. And they apparently knew all about her and Jack. But how?

Italia continued, "We're gonna make sure no one ever finds your body, and if they do, they ain't gonna recognize you."

The words terrified Lauren.

And Italia's language was suddenly street-like instead of refined. Which one was the real Italia?

"Please. Please. I'm so sorry. I promise to never..." Lauren begged.

"Shut up, Bitch!" screamed Italia. "I want you to see what I have in this envelope." She started to spread out each of the twelve enlargements on the kitchen table. "Take a look at this one. And this one." She continued until all twelve were displayed.

Lauren glimpsed at the scenes captured in the photos and asked in trepidation, "Where did you get these?" She was horrified to see so many of her tenderest moments with Jack from the night before. The moments that meant so much to both of them. Moments that would stay with her until her death.

"What does it matter? That's you, isn't it? With Jack. You're going to pay for this." Italia's eyes started to well up with tears. "I trusted you. I loved you. I can't believe you betrayed me."

Lauren thought, *"Who tries to kill someone they love! She must be sick! And didn't she betray Jack when she seduced her?"* Then another thought went through her mind, *"And didn't I betray Jack, too, when I had sex with his wife?"* She felt enormous guilt for her very bad decision.

"Where is Jack?" Lauren asked, fearing that they had killed him when he arrived home from the police station.

"You tell me!" yelled Italia with a crazed look in her eyes. "Is he here?" She looked around. "Did he stay here with you last night?" She left Tony pointing his gun at Lauren in the kitchen while she went to every room and tore apart every hiding spot in the closets, the basement, the garage, and the car. She didn't find Jack after 15 minutes of searching.

"He's not here, I tell you!" claimed Lauren. "The police took him to headquarters last night."

Tony was startled. "Headquarters? Suppose you tell me what they said?" He poked the gun in her ribs.

"The FBI wouldn't explain the reason for detaining him. They said they would explain everything at the police station."

"FBI??" Tony was showing signs of nervousness. "Did they mention my name? Tell me now!" He hit her face with the butt of the gun and she fell on the kitchen floor in pain.

"They didn't mention your name!! I swear!" She raised her hand in front of her face to block another blow.

"Italia! Look. We gotta make this fast. I have to leave town," Tony insisted. "See how much money she has in her purse."

Italia found the purse and pulled out her wallet. "$200. She won't need it anymore." She handed it to Tony, who put it in his pocket.

The cash changing hands made Italia think about the money she had hidden away at home. If she needed to get away, she'd also need that cash. "Anthony, you know what you need to do here. I have to take the car back to the house for a few minutes. I forgot to do something. I won't be long. I'll be back for you in 30 to pick you up. Don't worry. No one knows we're here." Then she looked at Lauren and said in a cold, unforgiving voice, "It could have been wonderful, but you had to go and ruin everything. Goodbye, Lauren."

"Italia! Please!" Lauren pleaded with both her words and her facial expression.

Italia looked at her brother and added, "Make it quick."

She took the key fob from Tony and left in the Range Rover, speeding by Sue's parked car. Sue saw that it was Jack's wife who was driving. Where was her brother? And, more importantly, where was Lauren?

Inside the kitchen, Lauren was afraid of what Tony might do to her. He could outright kill her...He could beat her...He could rape her. Or all three. And no one in the world knew the danger she was in. There was no one to save her. She was terrified. She didn't want to die. Especially not like this. She prayed to God, asking Him to forgive her for going after Italia's husband. *"What have I done?"* she thought with sincere regret. However, she knew that she would always have love in her heart for Jack, even though their time together on this earth was very short.

Tony was also considering what he was going to do. He knew he was going to kill her, but he had thirty minutes until Italia got back. He couldn't go anywhere until then, so why not take advantage of it? He felt very masterful with the gun in his hand. Very powerful. In control. In charge of her life and death. The saliva in his mouth increased as the fantasy of raping and beating her took over his mind. He knew what he wanted to do. He felt an erection in his pants as he envisioned this playing out. She would beg for mercy and he would hit her face until he broke some bones. If she fought him, he'd punch her again. Then he'd fuck her until she screamed. He'd show her! Then he thought about strangling her, rather than shooting her. It was much more personal, and enjoyable.

And he had time to kill.

"Get up, Bitch!" Tony ordered. Lauren slowly got herself up, feeling the massive bruise taking form on her cheek. He poked her with the gun barrel and pushed her towards the bedroom.

"Take your clothes off and get on the bed," he ordered. He felt the need to hurt her. Badly. To see her suffer. The urge was building up throughout his body and mind, taking over, until that's all he could think about was inflicting pain upon her, disfiguring her. His blood pressure was rising. His face was turning red with anger. He gritted his teeth and his lips formed a snarl as he stared at Lauren with sudden hatred. Yet, this hatred was like foreplay to a sexual climax. It was, indeed, a sexual desire, but one that had a sick twist. The release would come when he had control of her body...and her life and death. He was truly mad.

Lauren, whimpering, started to take off her top when she heard a sound like one explosion and then another much louder one! She let out a fearful cry. Tony quickly turned away from Lauren and braced himself against the bedroom wall with his gun ready to use.

"FBI! Anthony Marconi, come out with your hands up! We know you're in there!" demanded the voice.

Lauren dropped down to hide next to the bed in

case there was gunfire.

Tony lost his erection. The look on his face was shock at first, then anger, then determination. He was not going to give up easily.

Both Lauren and Tony heard multiple police sirens approaching the house and could see flashing red and blue lights shining through the windows. He looked out the bedroom window to the backyard and observed uniformed officers turning the corner of the house.

Tony broke a window with the gun and fired a warning shot at the officers.

Lauren heard the police yell, "Shots fired!" She covered her head with her hands.

Once again, the voice said, "FBI! Anthony Marconi, drop your weapon! Come out with your hands up! The house is surrounded. You cannot escape."

Tony identified at least two armed officers sheltering behind the trees. He had several choices and none of them were good. He could keep himself barricaded in the bedroom for hours. To what end? He needed to think! He could shoot the "bitch" out of spite, but that would not help his situation. In fact, the police might swarm the bedroom and kill him. He could pick off the officers one by one, but they had trained marksmen with bulletproof vests and bigger guns, and he wasn't that skilled at shooting. He briefly thought about "offing" himself but dismissed it. None of these would get him out of the small bedroom without a gun battle. There was nowhere to run. Italia had his car. He assumed that there were additional officers in the living room just waiting for him to make a move. He knew he was fucked. He also thought about "death by cop." But he still had a glimmer of hope—hope that his jail term would be relatively short, or he would be acquitted. Perhaps he could even escape!

He went back to the bedroom doorway and threw his gun into the hallway. He wasn't willing to die.

Immediately, two SWAT officers came in and took him down and cuffed him. He didn't resist.

Lauren called out, "Don't shoot. I'm on the floor." She did a face plant and spread her arms out, as a man stood above her. He wore brown dress shoes and brown dress pants. She looked up. It was Rennie! He held a hand out for her and she put her hand in his, as he helped her up. Lauren looked at him, confused. "Rennie? Um...thank you."

"Don't thank me. There's someone else you need to thank."

Lauren turned around and saw Sue, as she entered the room. "Sue? I don't understand!"

Sue hugged Lauren. "I told you I would be your eyes and ears. You're okay. That's all that matters."

Rennie, or Agent Sturr, continued, "We're going to have EMS check you out in a few minutes and then, perhaps, we can talk. Would that be alright?"

"Yes... Oh my God! Italia! She went back to her house and said she'd be back here in thirty minutes!" Lauren warned.

"We'll send some officers over there." He went outside and talked to Lt. Fitch who just arrived on the scene. Tony had been placed in the back seat of a police cruiser where he stared straight ahead, angry at himself for getting caught. He was under arrest for a litany of charges including aggravated assault, attempted murder, armed robbery, and possession of a stolen firearm, in addition to his warrants for sex trafficking, and second-degree murder in the death of the prostitute behind the Fox Den.

Lauren went into the living room and saw the busted front door with a large boot mark. *"A small price to pay,"* she thought. There was also a smoky remnant of the explosive breaching device the police used to gain entrance and stun the gunman, who, unfortunately, was in another room. She was shaking so she sat down on a side chair. There were officers milling in and out. The enlargements were still on the kitchen table, but she didn't have the strength to get up and collect them, and she assumed that they would be taken as evidence anyway, as embarrassing as they were.

Then she heard her name being called, so she turned around and saw Jack! He was alive! She stood up and he put his arms around her and hugged her for a long while. She never wanted to let him go. She wept freely on his shoulder and apologized for everything that happened.

"Shhh," he comforted her. "Are you okay? I was so worried!"

She started to tell him about Italia, but he told her that they would talk about her later when they had a private moment. He had been informed that his wife had been part of this, and he was shocked and confused at first, but somehow not surprised. They would both hear the entire story at some point.

Lauren said with a smile, "Jack, I want you to meet my administrative assistant, Sue, or should I say, Sue Gainer, Private Eye?"

Sue giggled and said hi, and Jack thanked her for saving Lauren's life.

The police took everyone's statement and bagged the gun and, unfortunately, the photos. Since the door still had to be replaced, they just propped it up and sealed it with tape. Lauren and Jack would deal with all the damage tomorrow.

Lauren didn't want to stay in the house after what she had been through.

"Stay at the beach house with me tonight," offered Jack. "I won't be going home either."

She agreed, and packed up a suitcase, including the green silk nightgown, which had already been pressed and returned to its store box.

23

Italia had no intention of returning for Tony. She knew he would kill Lauren sooner or later and she didn't want to witness it. Did she really feel love for Lauren, or did she just want to distance herself from the crime? Perhaps a little of both. She was also leaving Tony to fend for himself. He would be violently angry when he realized she wasn't coming back. She knew it, but she didn't care. Her life was essentially over anyway.

She wept as she drove, stopping at the house where Tony picked up a weapon earlier. She wanted a gun for herself. After she wiped her eyes, she climbed the rickety porch steps and knocked on the door twice, then another three times. That was the code. A skinny tattooed man, wearing an undershirt and jeans and with a cigarette hanging from his lips, answered the door, looking surprised at her presence. "I need a gun and some ammo." That's all she said. He ushered her into a dark and dingy living room.

"What are you looking for?" His eyes focused on her, wondering why a pretty lady such as this would need a weapon.

"The only gun I'm familiar with is a 9mm," she explained.

"Okay. I've got one, with one full magazine. $100. Special price just for you." He smiled and showed his yellow teeth from all the cigarette smoking.

"No problem." She handed over the money.

He retrieved a gun from a box, wrapped it in a cheap white towel, and handed it to her. "You know where to find me if you need, er, anything else." He smiled as he looked her over one more time.

She left without another word and went back to her car.

She was hoping Jack would be home when she got there.

He wasn't.

His truck was not in the garage or the driveway. She had planned to destroy him as he had destroyed her. She wanted to punish him. To take revenge out on him. To make him suffer. It was unfortunate that he couldn't see his beloved Lauren die in front of him to make him crazy. And now, she couldn't exact her revenge on him as she had planned by shooting him.

Livid, Italia went in the house holding the gun, just in case... When she was sure that Jack wasn't home, she went to her jewelry drawer where she had hidden cash over the years in a thick envelope and stuffed it into her purse, along with her gun. She also gathered a few clothes, putting them into her beach tote. Then she looked around the house, trying to decide what she could do to get her revenge on Jack.

When the doorbell rang, she was startled. Was it the police? Could it be Jack? She peeked out through the curtains and saw a casually dressed man she didn't know. She didn't recognize his car either. Could someone have more pictures of her betrayers? She was confused, but curious. Maybe he was just a salesman. She decided to answer the door. He could provide her with an alibi, as well. She could tell the police that she was home when her brother killed Lauren. It actually made sense to have this man see her.

When she opened the door, the man asked, "Italia Kenner?"

She replied, "Yes. Can I help you?"

"You are served," he replied and then handed her a folded packet of papers. He turned, walked down the steps, and got back into his car.

Italia opened up the packet to find that Jack had filed for divorce!

She freaked out. She slammed the door and stood there shaking in anger, disbelief, and unbearable hurt. *"How could he do this to me?"* she asked herself. Yet, a few minutes before, she had been looking for revenge and planned to kill him had he been home. It looked like he had the last laugh. She refused to let that happen. "Damn you, Jack!" she screamed upon deaf ears. "I will kill you if it's the last thing I do! I will destroy everything you love!"

Grabbing her purse and tote, she went into the garage to back out her Miata. Then she saw the red gas can sitting by the back wall of the garage. She parked her Miata in the driveway alongside the Range Rover and went back into the garage. Italia picked up the can, which was almost full, and carried it inside the house. In the kitchen, she found a pack of matches and put them in the pocket of her shorts. She began to splash the gasoline all over the first floor of the house. She turned on the gas in the fireplace, but turned off the flame. As she was leaving the doorway, she struck a match and lit the nearest puddle. The flames flew up immediately and followed the zig-zag of the drizzled gas. She closed the door and locked it.

No smoke alarms sounded, but when the whole house exploded, it shook the ground for at least a mile in all directions.

By then, Italia was on the road with her purse full of cash and her gun. She drove to the only place she could go—home. Home to her mother.

* * * * *

Sophia Marconi had been dusting the upstairs when she heard the doorbell. She assumed Dominic would answer the door, which he did, while she listened. She was a curious person; perhaps even a nosey person.

It was the Trenton police, looking for Italia! How odd! Dominic insisted that she wasn't there, but they demanded to search the premises anyway. After a futile search, they departed, with a warning. If Italia arrives and they don't notify the police, they will both be arrested for harboring a fugitive. Dominic slammed the door in their faces, after which he ranted and cursed in Italian for five minutes.

He would never, in any stretch of the imagination, ever, snitch on his daughter. *"What did she do, anyway?"* he wondered. *"Kill her good-for-nothing husband? Big fucking deal!"*

He went upstairs to find his wife. The carpeting was cushy and silent, and he approached without sound. What he saw stunned him. Sophia was rolling hundred-dollar bills and stuffing them into her socks! Slowly, he crept closer and saw the many socks in her drawer loaded with cash. Thousands of dollars! Of his money! He was angry beyond belief.

He grabbed her chubby arm and twisted it, surprising her and inflicting great pain. He exploded with anger, booming, "You fucking bitch! Stealing my hard-earned money!" He punched her in the face, once, then twice more, breaking her nose. The blood dripped onto the carpeting as well as the bedspread where she fell.

Sophia screamed continuously, but no one heard those screams. The 12-inch-thick stucco walls kept all the secrets inside. He continued to beat her, until she wasn't moving anymore. Her old and tired face was no longer recognizable. There was blood soaked into the bedspread and rug. He stopped and looked down at her, despising her very dead body. He went into their on-suite bathroom and washed his hands. He took off his bloody clothes and carried them to the laundry room on the first floor, where he ran the machines. Then, prepared with a black trash bag, he went back to where Sophia lay dead. He stepped over her body and removed all the socks from the drawer and put them into the trash bag. He would sort it all out later.

After he donned new clothing, he made a phone call to *"i suoi amici,"* his friends, Sammy and Marco. He needed a favor. Within an hour, the bathroom was cleaned with bleach, the bedspread and sheets were removed, and the body was placed into a cut section of the bloodied carpet, rolled up, and taken out to a van in the garage. There were deep woods about two hours away where they would dig Sophia's grave. Not to worry.

Dominic looked at his hands. The knuckles on his

right hand were torn up from all the punching and they hurt. *"How will I explain this, if I have to?"* he wondered nervously. He went into his garage and purposely re-injured his right hand on a workbench with a rusty saw blade, leaving his blood behind as evidence.

He went back into his house, thinking about the repercussions of what he had just done. He would have to shop at the grocery store, make his own meals, clean his house, and do the laundry. Maybe he shouldn't have gotten so angry. *"But she deserved it!"* he growled to himself and went back to his recliner to watch TV.

"I can always hire a maid!"

24

"Zucchini" Sam, named for his unforgettable dance with a zucchini between his legs, and Marco "the beast," named for his height and girth, rented a white panel van at Dominic's request, bought two shovels, two carpet cutters, and rope at Home Depot, and drove to the villa. There, Dominic met them at the door that adjoined the three-car garage, where they pulled in and turned off the engine. Dominic hit the remote and the *whirring* door closed with a final bang on the cement floor.

Sam was in the driver's seat, while Marco rode "shotgun." It took an extra minute for Marco to move his immense body out of the passenger seat, but that was not unusual. Once he was standing, he had to wait a minute for his body to align and to put weight on his hips. Bursitis, they told him. Someday he'd need a hip replacement, too. By the time he climbed the two wooden steps into the house, he was already sweating. He wiped his brow with a handkerchief from his pocket.

They both gave Dominic a "man hug," with a couple of pats on the back, as they had done hundreds of times before. They followed him through the house, up the stairs (with Marco lagging behind), and into the bedroom.

Sam winced at the sight. It was not what he was expecting to see—a bruised, bloody, and lifeless body of an old, chunky woman who was not immediately recognizable. Her housedress gave her away. It was Sophia—the often quiet, humble, and welcoming lady of the house, and the one who fed them well. Very well.

Marco looked at Dominic for an explanation, but there was none. His sweaty brow, now crossed with sadness and confusion, dripped onto the carpet.

"I need you guys to cut out all the stained carpet and take her carcass outta here," demanded Dominic in an angry, cold voice.

Sam and Marco exchanged glances then got to work, each with carpet cutters, slicing a large swath of carpet on each side of the body. They then rolled the body up and tied a rope on each end. Marco picked up one end, while Sam and Dominic lifted the other end together. They all stumbled and grunted as they carried their awkward load through the doorway and down the twenty steps, through the living room and kitchen, and through the small doorway to the garage, down the two wooden steps, and over to the van, where they put down the body and rested for a few moments. Sam opened the back of the van and jumped in. Marco picked up the nearest end of the rolled carpet and lifted it up, while Dominic struggled with the back end. Once they got the carpet part way in, Sam pulled as Marco pushed it in all way to the front of the van.

Breathless, all three returned to the house for water and another quick rest.

"You're not done yet," warned Dominic. "You gotta help me clean up."

Once again, they climbed the stairs to the second floor. Sam and Marco ripped out the rest of the carpet then cut it into smaller sections and took it out to the curb, where it would be picked up the next day. They returned to the bedroom again; this time to clean up the blood. Sam scoured the bathroom with bleach, while Marco was asked to take care of the bed.

Marco was visibly tired. Sweaty patches appeared under his arms and around his groin, and his body odor was noticeable to the two other men.

"God, Marco. You stink!" Dominic looked at him disgustedly. "What have you been eating?"

Marco, embarrassed, shrugged his shoulders, while Sam laughed. Then Marco let out a loud and stinky fart and the other two men stopped what they were doing to give him dirty looks.

Exhausted, Marco was no longer working as hard as he should have. He was supposed to flip the mattress, but he just covered it, along with the dried blood, with a clean sheet. He was supposed to check the rest of the room, too, but he didn't. Even so, Dominic never noticed the blood spatter here and there with his failing eyesight.

Soon, the three men returned to the garage. Dominic hit the remote and the garage door opened. Sam and Marco got into the van and backed out into the driveway.

"Don't worry, Dom. We'll take care of this. We know some woods south of the city. Nobody goes there," Sam assured. Dominic nodded and waved them on. He was tired and he hoped to God that they wouldn't screw this up.

Out on the highway, Marco, who was basking in the air conditioning, turned to Sam and asked, "What do you think happened there?"

"Maybe she said something that pissed him off, big time. Or maybe she was leaving him," Sam speculated.

"Maybe," considered Marco. "Or maybe he wanted some action and she had a headache." They both laughed.

"Well, she had a HUGE headache when he got done with her!" Sam added, still smiling.

"I feel bad, though. She was a nice lady," Marco lamented. "And, oh, that ravioli of hers was the best, wasn't it?" Marco thought about that for awhile. He could almost taste it. "Too bad."

They exited the highway and drove about a half mile on the county road to reach the woods. They turned onto a dirt road that went into the woods and drove until they could no longer see the county road. This dirt road was rarely used but Sam had been there before for other "jobs."

Opening the back of the van, they each grabbed a shovel. They closed the back door of the van, not bothering to lock it, and walked deep into the woods.

"I'm hungry," Marco said. "And tired. We shoudda got some take-out."

"Too late now. We gotta dig a hole and take care of business," Sam advised.

They chose a quiet spot without a lot of tree roots and began to dig—except that the dirt was rock hard. They expected sandy soil, but in this area, it was far from that.

"What the fuck?" complained Sam. "How are we gonna dig six feet?"

"I dunno," sighed Marco. "I'm beat!" He started to sweat again in the stagnant and stifling summer heat of the forest.

They stood there for a few minutes, each thinking that they didn't want to be doing this.

Marco spoke first. "What about we just cover her with debris?"

"We shouldn't...Dom's gonna be mad...but I don't know what else to do." Sam easily gave in.

There was another long pause as the men leaned on their shovels and continued to stare at the ground and contemplate what to do.

Sam decided, saying, "Fuck that asshole Dominic. Let's go get the body." They took the shovels back to the van, and pulled out the carpet with the dead body.

It was even more difficult for just two men to lug the rolled carpet to the site they had picked. Even with the rope, they tripped and dropped the carpet a few times, leaving a trail of loose fibers from the van to the dump site. Once they reached the spot, they untied the carpet, dropped the rope, and let the body roll out onto the ground. First, they covered the body with the carpet and then covered the carpet with leaves, branches, moss—anything they could find from the forest floor. When they were satisfied with how "natural" it looked, they headed back to the van.

Exhausted from their hard day's work, they drove to the truck rental company and dropped off the van, without cleaning it out or removing the shovels.

Marco commented, "Whew! That's done. Let's go eat."

Sam slapped his back and laughed. "Haha. They don't call you 'the beast' for nothin'. We deserve it! Don't we?" Moving his hips, he did his zucchini dance with an invisible zucchini. "Bada Bing!" They both laughed.

They walked to a nearby Italian restaurant and filled up on five different pasta dishes, bread, and other delicacies on the hot-and-cold, all-you-can-eat salad bar before calling an Uber for a ride home.

Later, a truck rental employee went to check the van and record the mileage and found the two shovels, dirt, and carpet fibers. However, he didn't think anything suspicious at the time. He put the shovels in a Lost & Found closet and swept out the van. But a week later, he got a call from the police who were checking up on a truck rental and he remembered two guys...

❧ *25* ❧

Three hours after the explosion at her home, Italia pulled up in her parents' driveway. She grabbed her purse and the tote and went up to the door. She never rang or knocked at her parents' home; she just walked in.

"Mama! Papa! It's Italia!" she announced, as she walked toward the kitchen. No Mama. It was awfully quiet, except for the sound of the TV in the living room. She went in there and found her father asleep in his recliner with the TV blaring a rerun of *Gunsmoke.* She shook his shoulder.

"Papa! Wake up! It's me, Italia!"

"Wha?" Dominic had been deep in sleep after the brutal murder of his wife and the strenuous work of carrying the body and disposal of the evidence. He was shocked to hear a feminine voice calling him. For a second, he thought it might be the ghost of Sophia coming back to haunt him. Maybe it was a dream. Maybe she was still alive and waking him for dinner.

Italia repeated, "Papa, wake up!" His eyes slowly opened, seeing the angelic face of his daughter.

"*La mia dolce bambina,*" he said softly in half-sleep.

"Yes, it's me. Where's Mama? Did she go out?"

Suddenly Dominic was awake and alert. He needed to think before he answered any questions. He needed to divert the attention to something else.

"Italia, the police were here earlier, looking for you. What have you done?"

Italia was shocked and speechless. She did not expect them to catch up to her already. She wondered what happened in Lauren's house? Did the gunfire alert the neighbors who called the police? Did Tony get caught and snitch on her? Or did he get away? How far could he go without a car? Perhaps the police were just trying to find out if she survived the fire at her house.

"Nothing, Papa. But I need to stay here for awhile. Where's Mama?" she said, bringing back the topic he was trying to avoid.

"She has a sick friend and went to stay with her for a few days. I guess we're on our own." He nervously laughed a little, his gray mustache twitching.

"Oh. I suppose I could cook something up for us to eat," she offered.

"That would be nice," he replied, thankful that she would feed him. At least tonight. He had no intention of calling the police about her arrival.

"Italia, put your car in the garage tonight. There have been some car burglaries."

"Okay, Papa."

She took care of that and then carried her tote to her childhood bedroom. Italia saw the door ajar to her parents' bedroom and the sight confused her. It looked like there was no carpeting. She walked in to see the furniture displaced somewhat, and just a bare wooden floor with carpet nails sticking up on a strip along the edge of the room.

Later, as they were eating some pasta, she asked her father about the carpeting.

He soothed her concerns. "It was time for new carpeting, and they will be installing a new one in a day or two. Fortunately, your mama doesn't have to put up with the workmen while she's gone." He chuckled.

It made sense to Italia.

When she saw the fresh wounds on his knuckles, she asked with sincere concern, "Oh, Papa! How did you hurt your hand?"

"Eh. I was at the workbench in the garage when I injured it on the saw. Don't you worry; it's fine."

"You have to be more careful!" she warned.

The next morning, after a breakfast of seasoned sliced tomatoes and eggs, Italia went back to her parents' room to gather the sheets for laundry. It was the least she could do while her mother was gone. However, neither her father nor his friends flipped the mattress where Sophia bled from her broken nose and beating; instead they just covered it with a clean sheet. Seeing blood startled Italia. It looked like a lot of blood. The spot was deep into the mattress. She looked up and saw blood spatter on the ceiling. And on the picture frame sitting on the dresser that held a picture of Tony and herself as small children. And tiny spots on the nearby walls. And on the leaves of a plant in the corner.

Fear sent chills down her spine. After she sat on the edge of the bed and caught her breath, she slowly went through several possible scenarios, none of which made sense. Only death made sense.

She discovered that her mother did not take any clothing, shoes, or jewelry to her visit with her sick friend. Nor did she take her purse. That was the clincher. Italia knew she was gone. Forever.

She closed her eyes, and silently wept. She said a prayer for her mother as she rocked back and forth on the mattress. Then she said a prayer for herself for what she was about to do. Italia had a lot on her conscience, but it wasn't going to stop her from taking care of things here. She left the laundry behind and went downstairs to remove the gun from her purse.

"Papa." She faced him as he sat watching the *Good Morning America* show, with the gun behind her back.

"Sh-h-h, you're in the way!" he complained. "I'm watching Lady Gaga talk about her new movie. That Lady Gaga is a real looker! Have you heard her sing with Tony Bennett?"

"Papa," she continued. "Where is Mama, really? Is she dead? Did you kill her?"

"Wha? You're crazy!" He dismissed the thought, but the gears in his brain were turning.

"I want the truth, Papa. What did she 'do' to you this time?"

Her direct question was enough to start him thinking. It was just enough to make him mad all over again. He was quiet for a minute, then started to voice his complaints.

"I found her stealing my money! My hard-earned money, and hiding it in her socks! I caught her! My money!"

"Then what, Papa?" Italia asked in a very quiet, cold tone. "What did you do to her? Where is she?"

Her father stared blankly, remembering what had

transpired, second by second, in that upstairs bedroom. After a minute or two, he started to weep. He covered his face with his aged, wrinkled hands and sobbed. "Yes, yes. I killed her," he cried. It was another minute before he spoke again. Looking at his daughter with his eyes wide and filled with craziness and rage, he suddenly burst out in cold anger, "She deserved it!"

Those were the last words he ever spoke. Italia drew the gun in front of her, pumped a round into the chamber, flipped off the safety and, remembering everything she learned at the range, shot him right between his eyes, just like she did with the target. But much, much closer. It blew the backside of his head into the recliner and a hole into the chair. He slumped to the side with his feet still raised on the footrest. She shot him again. This time she didn't bother to aim.

Italia suddenly felt exhausted. She sat down in another chair in the living room, still holding the gun loosely in her hand. She debated whether to use it on herself, but couldn't make that decision. She thought about Jack, her father, and her brother. She hated all the men in her life for destroying her life.

Her evil father killed her sweet, little, old mother, who raised her and her brother with much love and devotion, who slaved for him every day, and who quietly took regular beatings from him. So what if she put aside some money? She did herself. Every woman needs to have some independence, whether it's the freedom to go where she pleases, make her own decisions, or keep herself financially stable. Her mother did not have these opportunities, or so she thought. In her heart, Italia was proud that her mother had enough sense to stash money away for a "rainy day." But where did it get her? Dead.

Yet, Italia promised to protect her mother, and she failed to arrive in time. It crushed her to know that she let her down. She should have forced her to live with her and Jack—except there was no home to go to anymore. She hadn't thought of that. It was a moot point now. No mother. No house. And the dead body of her father sitting across the room from her. Again, Italia wept until her mascara streaked down her tan cheeks.

Then there was Anthony, who also had a history of beating women. Italia wasn't fooled by him. She knew his involvement with prostitutes and she suspected that he coerced young girls into the trade, the sex trade, sometimes taking them against their will. A way for him to make goddamn money. It was disgusting. Once, when she was 13, he even tried to have sex with her, until she clubbed him with a fireplace poker and made his head bleed. She hoped he rotted in hell. She felt no remorse for leaving him behind at Lauren's. She chuckled at the thought of Anthony getting very anxious with no one to get him away from the scene of the crime and no car to escape in.

And then there was Jack. The only man she had ever loved and trusted. Now she hated him. He had the nerve to steal Lauren from her. She totally blamed him for Lauren's death. She was sure she was dead by now. If it weren't for Jack's debauchery, Lauren would still be her lover. And she would still be alive. It was all his fault. He flirted with a lot of women and they acted so coy around him. Bastard! She wondered just how he seduced Lauren, and when. It made her so angry!

But the biggest shock to Italia was the serving of the divorce papers. She started to babble out loud to herself about everything in their married life and how she was the only one who worked at it. Jack did nothing after the honeymoon to keep their love alive. He just went to work every day. She had to come up with all the plans. She had to work to get his attention all the time. He hadn't loved her in a long time. Why? Italia knew it couldn't be her appearance, which, by all standards, was a "10." She was friendly and witty and sexy. Just ask Lauren who laughed with her and loved her! "Oh, I guess he can't ask Lauren. Anymore," she moaned as she grieved silently for her lover. More tears rolled down from her eyes and her nose ran from all the crying. She wiped her nose with the back of her hand.

She sat there for a long while, thinking about the tragedies that had taken place. She looked at the gun, still in her hand. *"Should I shoot myself and get it over with?"* she debated. Again, she held the gun up to her temple, but she couldn't pull the trigger. She put the gun back in her lap a second time.

"What should I do?" she wondered. She didn't want to bother hiding her crime. She would freely confess. After all, he murdered her mother. He was the evil one. Not her. He couldn't hurt anyone anymore.

Italia started to think about her mom. Did her mother suffer terribly? Did her father have help to dispose of her mutilated body? Were they the same friends who used to kiss her on the lips whenever they visited and laugh afterwards? Where did they take her mother? Did they throw her away like garbage? Did they take her out into the ocean and dump her overboard? Did they bury her remains in an unknown grave? Italia knew she would never find out. Ghosts don't speak. She should have made her father explain exactly what he did before she shot him. Too late now. Too late now.

Then there was Lauren. Her last lover. Her most exciting lover. A "Mona Lisa" smile came across her face when she thought about the lovemaking in Lauren's bed that night. She was divine! Italia actually believed that Lauren was a victim of Jack's penchant for sexy women. His choices led to Lauren's murder. Again, Italia wasn't there when Anthony snuffed Lauren out so she didn't have a guilty conscience about the murder. Jack and Anthony. They were the guilty ones.

Italia began to dwell on the house fire. She gleefully destroyed all of Jack's worldly possessions, except his damn pickup truck. And she regretted that he didn't burn up with the house. She thought about the day when the egg exploded in the kitchen and smoke filled the downstairs. She laughed out loud. She did it on purpose. The problem was that she was hoping the whole damn house would catch on fire while she sat musing in the garden, but it didn't. Jack discovered it too soon. But he never discovered...

In the middle of her reverie, there was a loud knock at the door. She knew by the intense pounding of someone's fist that it was the police. She made no attempt to go to the door and let them in. Instead, she just sat there listlessly, holding the gun with no intention of using it.

When they eventually entered by force, the well-armed team pointed their AK-47s at her, ordering her to drop the gun. She looked up at them and laughed, "The batteries. I took out all the batteries! Jack should have had the alarm system hard-wired." She laughed again at her own joke.

They ordered her to drop the gun a second time. She let it fall to the carpet, and the team leader was upon it immediately and kicked it out of her reach. Italia was given her Miranda rights and arrested. Before she left the living room, she cursed her father in Italian for her mother's death. It gave her satisfaction and made her feel a little better.

✘ *26* ✘

Italia rode in the police car, in handcuffs, to the Trenton Police Department (TPD). There, she was "processed." In other words, she was fingerprinted (recorded into AFIS, the Automated Fingerprint Identification System), searched for tattoos, photographed, and given a blood test for DNA and any other lab work requested by the arresting officer. A female police officer had her strip down for the notorious visual strip search for possible weapons or drugs hidden in bodily cavities, and then sprayed her with an insecticide in case she had lice or any other infestation. Italia was then given an orange jump suit to wear to clearly identify her as an inmate of the Central Reception and Assignment Facility, better known as CRAF, which housed about 550 or so inmates of mixed security levels. It would be her first stop to a lifetime of hell.

Before she was sent to the facility, she had to be questioned by the TPD. She was escorted to an interrogation room at police headquarters. Handcuffs were not sufficient; due to the severity of her crimes, she was also chained around her ankles to a ring bolted to the floor. She sat and waited for her interrogator to walk in. There was nothing to look at except a table and a couple of chairs. She spotted a camera in the corner of the room. Normally, Italia would have given her best model's pose, but not today.

Meanwhile, outside of the interrogation room was another room where one, or several detectives could watch a prisoner's, suspect's, or witness' every move on a closed-caption-television screen, listen carefully to every word while it was being recorded on sophisticated equipment, and look for every nuance of a lie. The detective who was to interrogate her was Detective Pete Lippa. He was trained to notice subtle eye movements, head placement, hand gestures, and more. He was also trained how to question a suspect.

Pete had two decades of experience in the Major Crimes Unit, a job he tried to leave behind when he went home to his family each night (if no murders were committed). His children were boys, 10 and 12, who never seemed to have enough time with their dad. His wife of 14 years was patient and held down the fort as best she could on her own. There was no guarantee that her husband would be home for dinner, for bed, or even live to see the next day. It was a great weight on her shoulders, but she loved him and the boys loved him, and that's all that mattered.

Lippa didn't enter the room right away. He and two other detectives, who would act as backups, watched her for awhile. Did she hold her head up, or down in shame? Was she crying or unemotional? Was she nervously wringing her hands? Did she attempt to sleep by putting her head down on the table? All of these things were important to the interrogator. After viewing her, he could make a determination on his approach to get her to confess.

Italia appeared to be a bit of a tough cookie. She held her head up in confidence, throwing her long, black hair back once or twice in a defiant gesture. She stared straight ahead, perhaps thinking about her crime. Or perhaps she had developed her own strategy to diminish her crime. None of that was new to Detective Lippa. This wasn't his first rodeo.

"Showtime," Lippa said to the other detectives. "Wish me luck."

"Good luck," the two detectives said back to him. Then one detective added jokingly, "We don't want to see her seduce you with her charms!" They both chuckled.

Lippa unlocked the door and walked in. He didn't say anything right away, but sat down and took a closer look at Italia. Her silky black hair was a bit tousled; her mascara was mostly under her eyes after crying; and her French fingernails were still neatly painted a bright red. She really was a beautiful woman. On the outside. What was she like on the inside?

He started the conversation by being friendly, almost like meeting a girl for the first time. "Hello, I'm Pete Lippa and I've been assigned to this case. How are you?"

"Okay," she said sadly.

"Do you know why you're here?"

She stared at him like a wounded animal which had no fight left. A small voice came out with a simple "Yes."

"You were given your Miranda rights, correct?"
"Yes."

"And you understand those rights?"

"Yes."

"Are you willing to speak to me?"

"Yes."

Detective Lippa's entire body relaxed. He had her permission to interrogate her and that was a relief. The other detectives watching on the monitors let out a couple yelps. "She's gonna talk!" one said gleefully.

Lippa paused, then watched her face as he asked, "Can you tell me what you did and where you went Sunday and Monday of this week?"

She tensed up and her eyes looked downward and to the left. She was ashamed, but of what? Would she tell the truth?

She cleared her throat. "Well, I was at home with Anthony—that's my brother—when someone came to the door. Anthony was upstairs trying to find some pants to wear. Well, as I said, this strange guy showed up at my door. He had pictures of Jack, my husband, with my girlfriend."

"And who is your girlfriend?" Pete asked.

"Lauren Miller."

"Were they incriminating pictures?"

"Yes. They were making love. I was furious. The guy wanted $10,000 for those pictures and I ended up giving it to him. Later, I told Anthony, and he said he would 'take care' of them for me."

Detective Lippa asked, "Did he mean take care of the blackmailer? The pictures? Or your husband and girlfriend?"

"Husband, yeah. We drove to my girlfriend's house and I showed her the pictures."

"What did she say?"

"She asked where I got 'em. I said it didn't matter.

I screamed that she and Jack betrayed me!" Italia then began to sob. "I didn't mean for Anthony to kill her. I'm so sorry!"

It was apparent that Italia didn't know that Lauren was alive. He asked, "So, you just expected him to rough her up?"

"I just wanted Anthony to scare her. I loved Lauren!"

This was getting a bit confusing for Lippa, so he had to back up. "What do you mean, you loved Lauren?"

"She was my lover, dammit!" Italia shouted vehemently. *"Doesn't he understand?"* she thought.

He tried hard not to act surprised. "And she was Mr. Kenner's lover, too? Were you jealous?"

"Yes! I thought he was at her house, but I didn't find him. Anthony was going to rough him up, too."

"So, then what?"

"I left Anthony there and went home to see if Jack was there."

"Why did you leave your brother at Ms. Miller's?"

"I told him I'd be back in 30 minutes to pick him up."

"Did you go straight home?"

She didn't respond right away, so he knew that she was covering up something.

"Yes," she lied. She didn't want to reveal the gun purchase unless she had to.

"Okay, you're at your house. What then?"

She didn't want to tell him about the divorce papers, so she skipped that part of the story. She'd keep that for the lawyer.

"I grabbed some things, switched cars, and drove

to my parents' house."

"What about Anthony?"

"I went without him. He said he was going to skip town. He took Lauren's cash."

"What else did you do at your house?"

She shook her head. She wasn't going to confess to arson.

"So how did your house catch fire?"

"My house caught fire?" Her bottom lip was trembling, as her eyes looked away, as she played dumb.

"You didn't know?"

"No. Was Jack there?"

"I'm only concerned with your whereabouts." He wasn't going to reveal that Jack was being held by the Delaware police for questioning. "So, you drove to your parents' house."

"Yes. Mama wasn't there, but Papa was. He told me that Mama was visiting a sick friend. The next day I discovered that all of my mother's belongings, like her purse, were still in the house, and there was blood all over the bedroom. And the carpet had been removed. I noticed Papa's hand was injured. I asked Papa what he did to her. He said he killed her because she stole his money."

Detective Lippa remembered the bag full of cash. Here was the motive in her mother's death. And the murderer identified. Now they just needed the body.

"What happened then?"

"I was afraid, now that I knew what he had done, that he would kill me, too," she lied again. "I couldn't let that happen."

Lippa suspected that she was diminishing her role

in the crime, but he continued, "What did you do?"

"I shot him. Twice." Italia finally looked Detective Lippa in the eyes. No remorse there, he noted. It was chilling, even for a seasoned detective.

The two detectives in the other room let out a cheer and gave each other high-fives. "She admitted it!"

"Where'd you get the gun?" Lippa inquired.

She sighed. "I bought it from some guy over on Washington Street," she admitted.

Lippa ordered her to stand up. "Italia Kenner, you are charged with the murder of your father." He unchained her from the floor ring, made sure her hands were behind her back, and told her to go to the door, which he unlocked and opened.

"Not Lauren?"

"Lauren Miller is not dead. You may have an additional charge of attempted murder from the D.A. in Delaware."

Shock registered on her face and she gasped. Then she wept, with no way to wipe away the tears or blow her nose. *"Lauren is alive!"* she thought joyously. *"Thank God, she's alive!"*

Then she wondered, *"So, if Tony didn't kill her, where is Tony?"* That question remained unanswered, at least for now, but did she really want to know? Did she care? Perhaps he was dead. She didn't sense "loss" but she did feel sorry for herself. Her whole family was gone. She only had Jack and Lauren and she tried to kill them. What a mess she had made of her life!

Memories were all she had left now. She thought back to when she was a child. Some were happy times; some were cruel times. Her happiest moments were receiving all those pretty little gifts from Papa. They would always be wrapped in colorful paper with a large bow. And then there were the terrible, frightening times—again with Papa, when he was beating her mother. How could one person be so kind and then snap? She started laughing to herself. Isn't that what she did? Yes, she snapped. She made a mental note to mention that to her lawyer. She'd have to ask for public counsel unless Jack got her a good lawyer.

She also had her memory of Lauren and their lovemaking. It would help her survive. Perhaps she would forget over time, or it just wouldn't matter.

Lippa led her to the elevator, went up three flights, and headed for the lockup until they were ready to transport her to the Receiving Facility.

Italia didn't know what awaited her in jail. She knew it wouldn't be pleasant. When she was placed in the CRAF van, her entire body started to tremble, until a little urine was released. It was very humiliating, but this was only the start of her new normal. She was terrified. She wished she were dead. She knew now that she should have used that gun on herself. "Too late now. Too late now," she repeated sadly, as she sat with several other forlorn women in the van as they drove to the Receiving Facility to await trial.

There was one middle-aged woman who watched Italia with interest. "Your first time?" she asked.

"Yes. And you?"

"Second time. You're nervous, aren't you?"

A tear rolled down Italia's cheek.

"Don't worry, honey. You're awfully pretty. We're gonna take care of you."

Italia's chin dropped a little. What did she mean? She looked at the woman curiously. The woman grinned, snickered, and nodded her head. "Oh yeah, we'll take real good care of you."

* * * * *

This was, indeed, a complicated case. Detective Lippa knew full well that he and his team would need a lot more evidence to have her convicted, but they had a great start with the confession. He hoped to hear from the feds about Tony's confession, if there was one. If their stories collaborated, he would have enough for an indictment against her. Then it was up to the D.A. to prove the case and get a conviction, and for her lawyer to prove otherwise.

He sat back in his office chair and closed the folder in front of him. Then he called his wife and said he'd be home for dinner—for a change.

27

After Italia was booked in New Jersey, and Anthony Marconi was booked locally in Delaware, Lieutenant Fitch met in his office with Detective White and also Detective Lippa from the TPD. Since the crime crossed state lines, the two jurisdictions decided to work jointly. Lt. Fitch took the lead in the case of the missing woman, Sophia Marconi, because the workload in Trenton was much heavier.

"What's your take on the missing woman?" Fitch asked his team, as he leaned forward on his well-worn desk.

Detective Lippa replied, "The evidence indicates that someone was severely injured or murdered in the bedroom. As you know, the carpet was removed before Dominic Marconi was killed. We are checking the landfill for any carpet disposals from the most recent pickup in the Marconi neighborhood."

"Good. As soon as you learn something, let us know. What else?"

"We still don't have a body. She could be in the landfill with the carpet. Or, she could be somewhere else. Let's hope the body's not in the Atlantic."

Fitch nodded in agreement. "Have you canvassed

the neighborhood for CCTV cameras or witnesses?"

"Well, the Marconi property doesn't have a security camera and it's fairly secluded. There are no cameras pointing directly at their house or driveway. However, we are checking the footage from one privately operated camera on the street. It will show the cars coming or going on any particular day this week. That's a lot of hours for our guys to watch!"

"I'd suggest you put two guys on shift. We need to see if there's anything suspicious, like the same vehicle going to and from the Marconi property."

"Will do. We have two detectives going door to door to find out if anyone heard a shot or saw anything unusual in the last two or three days."

Detective Lippa continued, "After interrogating Mrs. Kenner, she said that the carpet had been removed before her visit and her father told her that her mother was visiting a sick friend. We know, for certain, that there was no sick friend. Mrs. Marconi was probably dead by then."

"Alright. That tells us two things. First, Mrs. Kenner is probably not the perpetrator in this missing person and probable homicide case. And secondly, we know that trash was picked up the day before Mrs. Kenner went to the house, so let's focus on the day before trash pickup until Mrs. Kenner's arrival."

Detective White made a suggestion. "I'd like to interview the known acquaintances of Dominic Marconi and Anthony Marconi to see what we can find out what they know or if they had any part in this."

"Do it," said Fitch.

Lippa added, "The body does not appear to be buried on the Marconi property, so it had to be removed. We obtained a warrant to search the Marconi car and Mrs. Kenner's car, but there was no trace evidence in either vehicle, so there has to be another vehicle involved."

They all thought about that for a few moments.

Fitch commented, "Let's check with car and truck rental companies."

Detective Lippa jotted it down. He would make some calls around Trenton.

"There's one more thing," interjected Lippa.

"What's that?"

"We searched the Marconi house and found a plastic trash bag full of hundred-dollar bills wrapped up in women's socks. Could be the motive."

"Looks that way. But let's not jump to conclusions. Let the facts talk for themselves."

They reviewed pictures from the crime scene, including the living room, bedroom, the trash bag of socks and money, and the trail of carpet fibers leading to the garage. They also discussed the 9mm gun in Italia's possession.

"Italia Kenner has been cooperative and has given us the description of the gun dealer and the house he works out of. He's a 'frequent flyer' here with multiple arrests. We need to bring him in for questioning." He handed White a printout of the dealer's record, most recent mug shot, and address.

White said he and his team would pick him up.

Lippa stood and shook Fitch's hand, then White's, as he prepared to depart. "We'll get started at our end," he promised.

"Thanks. Keep us informed," Fitch added.

After Lippa left, Lt. Fitch turned to Detective White.

"The family of Sheree Ramsey has been notified that the suspect in the case has been arrested. We have Miss Miller and Mr. Kenner coming in this afternoon to make their statements. If there are any updates between now and then, I'd like to hear about it. Otherwise, I'll see you this afternoon."

"Yes, sir."

❧ *28* ❧

Jack and Lauren sat in the conference room at the police station, holding hands beneath the table. Also present were Lt. Fitch, Detective White, and Agent Sturr.

"Jack," Agent Sturr began. "We never pinned you for the killer." He paused. "But we needed you to lead us to Tony and the evidence to prosecute. He was our focus from the start."

Lauren squeezed Jack's hand.

He continued, "Tony's activity in the sex trade is well documented. We had a Federal warrant for his arrest, but when he 'allegedly' killed the prostitute here, we held off on his arrest to obtain more evidence that would lock him away for many more years. We followed him from Trenton; we knew he was headed to your home and his sister. We figured he'd hole up there for awhile."

"I heard you guys came to the house looking for me, though," Jack mentioned.

Sturr responded, "First and foremost, we needed the gun. While we were at it, we picked up Tony's beer bottle to match to the DNA on the bottle we found in the dumpster at the Fox Den. The computer, which you can have back, by the way, was checked, but no usable evidence was found on it."

Now Lauren had a question. "Where has Italia been through all of this? She didn't come back to my house. Or did she?"

Fitch replied, "No. She is in custody."

He turned to Jack. "Mrs. Kenner and her brother went to Lauren's to confront her with the revealing pictures of the two of you from the house on Route 1."

Jack closed his eyes and briefly covered his face with his hands. "I saw them on Lauren's table last night. I was sick to think that Italia saw those pictures."

Lauren put her arm around him, and tried to comfort him. "I was shocked, too. Italia was livid, of course. I can't imagine how much grief they caused her."

"Where did they come from? Who took them?" Jack asked.

"I don't know!" Lauren replied. They both looked at Lt. Fitch for answers.

"We'll get to that in a minute. Miss Miller, we need a statement from you about what happened yesterday, from the time Mrs. Kenner and Anthony Marconi arrived at your door."

Lauren wrote down everything she could remember.

"Jack, I told Italia that I didn't know where you were. Shortly after that, she left my house to go back to your house—she said she forgot something, leaving Tony to kill me."

For Jack, this was very disturbing. How close Lauren came to being killed! By his own brother-in-law!

Fitch added to the story, "Jack, your wife told us that, after she purchased a gun from the same dealer her brother used, she went home to confront you, but luckily you were still in our custody."

Jack was even more shaken by this news, as he exchanged glances with Lauren. He recalled how good Italia was at the gun range. He had no doubt that she would have killed him had he been home. For once, he was thankful that he had been at police headquarters.

White interrupted. "Then, when the Trenton Police Department caught up with your wife at her father's house, she was sitting across the room from the body of her father with the gun in her hand. We did a ballistics test today and it was the murder weapon. It also appears that there was a second crime scene in the upstairs bedroom. We haven't found Sophia Marconi yet. It doesn't look good, but we haven't finished our investigation."

Jack was taken aback. He shook his head in disgust and his face revealed the anguish he was feeling. After all, they were his in-laws. Everything had to be sorted out—who killed whom and why. He couldn't even start to imagine why Italia would have done this. Did she go mad after seeing those pictures? Why would she kill her parents? Or did she? Perhaps she just picked the gun off the floor.

"And what will happen to Italia?" Jack asked with a concerned voice.

"She'll stand trial on multiple charges. She may be extradited to Delaware after her trial in Jersey," Lt. Fitch interjected.

Jack wanted to make sure she got a good defense

lawyer. Despite the fact that she might have killed him, he believed that she deserved a fair trial.

Lauren knew that she'd have to have a heart-to-heart discussion with Jack. There was so much he didn't know! She needed to tell him everything that happened between Italia and herself before the trial started. She owed him that. It was all going to come out anyway when they heard Italia's motives, and if it meant the end of her relationship with Jack, then that was meant to be, even though her heart would be broken. She knew she was responsible for her part with both Italia and Jack—which led to this perfect disaster. If he could understand Italia's mindset, and her own weakness, perhaps he could get past it and forgive her sin of passion. Italia may never forgive her, though, and she would have to live with that. She gave in to her own lustful desires and made love to both Italia and Jack, without regard for the other spouse. It was a love triangle of the worst kind. She had thrown herself at Jack after the kiss in the bar. It was that foolish and dangerous decision, she felt, which led to all this. She was ashamed of her actions and her deceit. But here was Jack, sitting next to her, naive of what really happened, and loving her. She hoped that he would continue to love her. She just wasn't sure... If he did stay with her, she promised to love him, and be true to him, forever.

Jack knew a little bit of Italia's love-hate relationship with her father. He also knew that there was a lot of drama, and perhaps abuse, in that family, as well. What made Italia shoot her father, if she did, he didn't know. He still loved her for the happy part of the life they shared together. He wanted her to be happy in life, too. He certainly never expected her to end up like this—in jail, with her father dead, her mother missing and most likely dead, and her brother in federal custody. Jack couldn't fathom how all this happened. It saddened him greatly. He also felt responsibility with his decision to have Lauren meet him at the beach house and have an affair. He started it! If he hadn't flirted with Lauren in that bar, none of this would have happened. And those pictures played a big part in Italia's crime against Lauren. Tony could have killed her! Jack shook his head in shame. Would he have done it all over again? He didn't know. Guilt laid heavily on his shoulders. All he knew, deep in his heart, was that he was falling in love with Lauren and wanted to protect her from all harm. Thank God, she was sitting next to him now, holding his hand, safe and sound. He hoped that she would forgive him for getting her involved in this mess. At least now they both had each other to lean on. He promised himself that he would always take care of her, no matter what, and love her forever. He was looking forward to a bright future with her.

Coming back into the present, Jack still had a lot of questions for the police.

"And the house? I heard there was a fire," Jack queried.

"I'm afraid your house is gone. We believe your wife set off a gas explosion. We were able to seize the Range Rover, which was left in the driveway far enough from the house, minus its windows. The lab will go over it today."

"Oh, my God!" he responded in disbelief. Shaken and shocked at this news, Jack looked at Lauren, who was also aghast, and then back at the detectives. Finally, when he regained his composure, he revealed, "It never was my house. Sure, my stuff was in there, but Italia's father bought the house for her. My name was never on the deed. That's why I bought the beach house. Something to call my own. I thought Italia and I would enjoy it someday, but she never got to see it."

Agent Sturr cracked a smile. "You had us surprised about that, too, Jack. If you hadn't given Lauren your beach address in an e-mail, we never would have known about it."

"E-mail?" Jack's brows furrowed.

"We had search warrants to monitor your correspondence and phone communications to find out what Tony might be up to and obtain evidence against him. Beeler allowed us to use their office space to set up operations close by. The taps have now been removed."

A light bulb seemingly went off in Lauren's head. "Oh, so that's what you were doing in your office! No one knew."

"No one, except Miss 'Nosey' Sue Gainer!" Agent Sturr laughed along with everyone else. "She had a bead on me almost from Day One. I don't know what made her follow me, but I had to lose her or else give myself away, and I couldn't risk that. It was too early in the game."

"Well, Rennie... Oh, that's not your name, is it? Sorry. Agent Sturr." Lauren apologized. "Sue told me she'd be my eyes and ears because I was having issues with my ex-husband."

"Tell us about that," asked Detective White, as he jotted some notes.

"My ex-husband, Phil. He's always trying to get money from me, but this time I refused to give it to him, so he went to the Kenner's house and asked Jack for money."

"Blackmail, pure and simple. He said he'd tell Italia about us, so I gave the money to him. I told him to never return," Jack informed everyone, believing that Phil would actually stay away.

The detective replied, "Well, let's see what we can do about him. After we're done here, Lauren, stop by my desk and give me a statement about Phil. We'll put a little pressure on your ex. It sounds like he needs to enjoy a little jail time."

Lauren and Jack smiled. Phil deserved a little police persuasion.

Lt. Fitch spoke up. "Which brings us back to the pictures. We have reason to believe that he's the one who took those pictures of you at the beach house and sold them to Mrs. Kenner."

"What? How did he know we were there?" Lauren asked, incredulous, with a blush coming over her face.

"He had to have followed you there. Miss Gainer gave us a description of a man taking photos through the window and he meets that description," Fitch said.

As he banged his fist on the table, Jack spouted, "That son of a bitch!"

"Let us take care of him," Fitch offered. "For starters, file an Order of Protection against Phil today. Both of you." They both nodded, as they stood up getting ready to leave the conference room. The next few months would be difficult, but at least they'd be facing it together.

* * * * *

At that moment, Phil was on a bumpy plane ride to Colombia, South America, with over ten thousand dollars in cash in his pocket and a shot of whiskey in his hand that he tossed down his throat, feeling the burn.

He grinned as he thought about the last forty-eight hours and how he tracked Lauren to the beach house. He had an app on his phone that tracked her every location, as long as her phone was turned on. It was as simple as that.

Now he had a new plan. He realized that he could live cheaply in Colombia, and he had "connections" who would pay him a steady income for a little trafficking. Life was going to be good. At least for awhile.

❧ *29* ❧

Seventy-two-year-old Martha Winger, whose name was appropriate for her hobby, was birdwatching in the woods south of Trenton in mid-August. Although it was hot, she wore a long-sleeved shirt and long pants tucked in her walking boots, a scarf around her neck, and a brimmed hat. Nesting season was over and many migrating birds were heading south, but she enjoyed going into the woods anyway. She lived alone after her husband passed away eight years before, and birdwatching gave her something to do on a regular basis. There were always woodpeckers and even a hawk or two to catch sight of. She wrote all her sightings down on a small spiral notepad (as she wasn't familiar with online note-taking or phone dictation), carefully dating each page.

Once in awhile, especially in April and early May, she'd run into other birders looking for warblers and other migrant birds. She knew almost all of the birders by name. Some were there to photograph the birds in low shrubs, while others aimed their binoculars high into the trees, often getting what is laughingly called "warbler neck," a painful condition from bending their neck backwards for long periods of time.

About ten days before, she saw a strange white van parked on the dirt road next to the woods. She thought it was odd, because there was a small parking area up the trail a bit that she and her birder friends normally used. She hadn't seen the van before or since, but she never gave it much thought again. Until today.

Today, she was in the same area of the woods where she had seen the van. Suddenly, she was aware of a foul odor. So foul that Martha started gagging and had to cover her mouth. Rather than go back in the direction of her car, she walked closer to the source of the smell. She thought it might be a dead deer, perhaps hit by a car and making it as far as the woods before collapsing. The closer she got, the more flies she encountered. Luckily, she had sprayed herself with a "deep woods" insect spray, primarily to keep away the ticks and black flies.

To her left, she spied a pile of debris. It looked a little unnatural, humped in a somewhat long manner. Flies were abundant on this hump. She began to clear away some of the branches, dead leaves, pine needles, moss, and dirt.

"What the heck?" she said aloud when she removed all the debris. "Why is there a carpet here? Why would anyone dump it in our nice woods? Those bastards!" She was angry that someone would use the woods as a dump site for their old, dirty carpet.

She lifted one corner of the carpet and immediately dropped it, as she recoiled in horror. Whatever it was, it was something gross that looked greenish and reddish in color and was covered in maggots. She couldn't tell if it had been a human being, but she wasn't going to look at it again.

Martha ran back to her car as fast as her arthritic feet could carry her. Her hands shook as she retrieved a cell phone from the center console. She was relieved to see that it had a signal. She punched in 911 on the oversized keypad.

"911. What is the source of your emergency?" the female voice said on the other end.

"I found something dead in the woods. Not sure if it's human, but it smells real bad."

"So, it might be human?" the operator questioned.

"Very possibly."

The 911 operator typed up the information into her computer and said a police unit was dispatched and would arrive shortly. Martha started the car, locked the doors, and ran the air conditioner, but she couldn't get the smell out of her nose.

* * * * *

Detective White knocked on Lt. Fitch's door. Fitch looked up and asked, "What's up?"

"Lippa called. A body was found south of Trenton. It could be our 'vic.'"

"We need to go," Fitch said, standing and grabbing his gray suit coat from the back of his chair.

They arrived in about two hours. The Trenton CSI team was still at work. Fitch and White saw Detective Lippa and ducked under the yellow crime-scene tape to enter the area. The smell was all too familiar...

Fitch asked, "What do you have?"

Lippa responded, "They are human remains in advanced stage of decomposition. Found by a woman walking in the woods. Get this: it was under a carpet."

Fitch exchanged glances with White. They would have to wait for the autopsy results before coming to a conclusion, but all signs pointed to Sophia Marconi.

"Anything else?"

"Well, the team found a trail of beige carpet fibers and followed it back to the dirt road. We can't determine what kind of vehicle was parked there because it's been too long and we've had rain. The woman who found the body is sitting in her car in the parking lot. She gave us a quick statement but you may want to interview her."

Fitch nodded and he and Detective White headed in her direction.

Martha was hoping she could leave soon, as her bladder was full and she couldn't hold it as long as she used to. She saw two men in suits walking toward her car. One man tapped on the window and she opened it all the way.

"Ms. Winger? I'm Lieutenant Fitch and this is Detective White. We're working on a case and wonder if you can help us out."

"Sure, as long as I can leave soon."

"That would be fine. I'm sure Detective Lippa has your name and address."

"Yes."

"Mind if we sit in your car?"

"Go ahead." She unlocked the car and they got in. Fitch sat in the front while White sat in the back. The air conditioning felt good.

"Could you tell us what happened today?" Lt. Fitch queried.

She told them what she experienced.

"Great. When was the last time you were here?"

"Well, I come every week, but I don't always walk the same trail. So, let's see..." She pulled out her notepad. "Oh, yes, I was here last Tuesday. I saw a yellow-rumped warbler, a pileated woodpecker, and a pair of wood ducks by the pond."

Fitch and White focused on the notepad. "Do you always write down your walks in your pad?"

"Sure! I have to keep track of the birds I see."

"The time before that...did you write down your sightings the week of August 5?"

"Um, yup. I was here August 5. Saw two downy woodpeckers, a red-tailed hawk, two turkey vultures, a blue-gray gnatcatcher, and a red-eyed vireo."

"Did you happen to see anything unusual that day? Besides birds." Fitch was getting excited. His heart was beating faster.

"Well, now that you mention it...There was a white van parked on the dirt road. You know, the kind that doesn't have any windows?" she posed as a question. "I wondered why the driver didn't park in the parking lot."

"Was there a company logo on the door or side?"

"Nope."

"Did you see the license plate?"

"Not really. I did recognize that it was a Jersey plate, though."

"Did you see the driver or a passenger?"

"Let me think...I kind of remember a big guy getting in the passenger side. Then they turned around and drove away. I didn't see any faces."

"You never saw the carpet dumped?"

"No! If I did, I would have yelled at the person who dumped it."

"You've been a big help, Miss Winger. Whatever you do, don't throw away that notepad."

"I keep all my notes, going back eight years."

"Wonderful. We'll be in touch. You can go now."

When Fitch and White got out of the car, Fitch slapped White on the back. "I have a feeling we're going to close this case soon!" They both grinned from ear to ear. "Now all we have to do is find that truck."

❧ *30* ❧

Detective Ralph Walsh of the Trenton Police Department was assigned to go through the surveillance videos from the Marconi case. It was a tedious job, trolling hours and hours of tape, and his eyes were tired from the intense viewing, trying to find something out of the ordinary on a well-traveled road.

After his seventh hour into it, he thought he saw something. He wasn't sure if it was his imagination. He played back the last 20 seconds. There! He played it back a second time. Yes, there! A white van driving south. He thought he saw the van earlier. He snapped a screen shot on the computer with a date and time stamp. Walsh went back two hours and kept hitting the arrow key to go frame by frame.

There it was—the same white van heading north. He zoomed in. He couldn't read the license plate, but it did look like two individuals in the front seat. He snapped another screen shot. He printed both shots out on the department's printer.

He went to Detective Lippa's desk. "Hey, I think I got something," he remarked. He showed him the two pictures.

"Good work, Ralph. I'll call Fitch." He made the call

and shared the pictures with Lt. Fitch through text.

Fitch banged his fist on the desk and said, "Yes!" He thanked Detective Lippa and walked over to White's desk. "Al, look at this."

Detective White stared at the photos. "I know this van. Let me check my notes." He flipped through his notepad, "Ah, here it is. Simmond's Truck Rental. I followed up on a possible lead. Two guys rented a van for the day. Left two shovels behind. I took a look at the van but didn't see anything suspicious. It was totally clean."

"We need those shovels to check for prints. And the van, of course."

"I'm on it." White took off immediately.

* * * * *

The turnaround time for testing DNA is rather lengthy for crime labs; it can take up to four months or longer in large cities. But fingerprint matching is much faster. The shovels were brought in along with fingerprints from the truck rental employee to rule him out. Once the shovels were dusted for prints, the prints were compared to other prints on record in AFIS. In a short amount of time, White had a hit.

"Samuel R. Mancuso," Detective White noted. "Booked in 1980 for racketeering and served 10 out of 20 years. Well, well, well. Hello, Sam! We'll be seeing you soon," he said with a chuckle.

Once again, Fitch and White drove to Trenton where they were met by Detective Lippa with the arrest warrant, and several members of his police force, who were ready for action. Lippa briefed his team, each with a particular duty.

* * * * *

"Zucchini" Sam heard about the murder of his *cumpari*, Dominic. To think that Dominic's own daughter killed him was beyond words. *"Everything he did for her! Everything he gave her! A house even! And this is the thanks he gets? I would kill her right now if she was here. Puttana!"* he thought angrily.

He found himself hitting the bottle a lot. He didn't eat. He just sat in his sleeveless white undershirt and plaid boxer shorts at his modest kitchen table looking out the window and thinking, *"How could this happen? I am so angry!"* He'd pour another shot. There was nothing else to think about; nothing else to do. Nothing else he *could* do.

He picked up the newspaper. The police had enough evidence to indict Italia and the grand jury agreed, as they handed down the indictment. "Thank God for that!" he stated vehemently. She would be in court tomorrow. He wanted to be sure Dominic got justice. He would be present to see it happen.

The next morning, he dressed in his best suit and tie. He indulged in one shot of whiskey before leaving the house. He had enough of a clear head to drive to the courtroom.

* * * * *

Lippa and his team carefully approached Samuel's house, according to protocol. Two officers went to the rear to create a perimeter. The lead enforcement officer banged three times on the door, and identified himself as police. No answer. They listened near the door and windows. They knocked again. None of the officers heard anything or saw anyone inside. After 15 minutes, Lippa decided that Samuel wasn't home. The team gathered to discuss whether or not there was a second address to go to. There wasn't. They would have to try again later.

* * * * *

Italia, in a modest blue suit rather than her prison garb, was led into the courtroom in handcuffs. She was frightened. But she still walked with grace and beauty. She turned to see who was there. Jack. And Lauren! Their eyes met for a moment and she saw tears in Lauren's eyes. Italia smiled at her. *"I'm so happy that she's still alive and I got to see her with my own eyes!"* she thought. Then she was instructed to sit at the table with her lawyer. The bailiff stood nearby to maintain a safe courtroom as he kept an eye on his prisoner. When the judge entered the room, everyone stood. To Italia, it was like a nightmare— something unreal. *"Is this really happening to me?"* she thought. *"I want to go home!"* But she knew she couldn't. First of all, there was no home to go to. She had destroyed it. She wanted to say she was sorry to Lauren. And to Jack. Jack hired a great lawyer for her; she might even get off! If not, perhaps one of them, or both of them, would visit her. She would like that. It was all she could hope for.

Her defense lawyer, a tall, immaculately dressed man, who had an excellent record of getting people off, told her that she had a "fairly good case," knowing that the police suspected her father of murdering her mother. His initial plan was to suggest "self-defense." If only her father hadn't been reclining in his chair! It was going to be hard to prove that he was a dangerous threat to her. Plan B was to have her plead insanity, but she brought the gun with her and her confession to police was cold and calculated. He didn't think the jury would buy "insanity." He would just have to do his best today to get an acquittal or the lowest possible sentence for her.

After the judge was seated, the rest of the courtroom sat as well. The clerk recited the docket number and case of Marconi vs. Kenner.

"How do you plead in the death of Dominic Marconi?" the judge asked the defendant.

"Not guilty," she said.

As soon as she spoke those words, her head fell to the table and her body slumped over. Her lawyer jumped up and away. The judge ducked behind the bench. Someone simultaneously yelled, "Gun!" and everyone started running from the courtroom.

Blood oozed from Italia's head. There were gasps from those who remained in the courtroom and some woman screamed. It was Lauren, who stood and leaned over the seat in front of her. Jack tried to pull her back down to her own seat so that she wouldn't be targeted as the next victim.

There, standing in the far-left corner at the rear of the courtroom, was a man in a suit—with a gun.

The bailiff ran to tackle the man. He didn't resist. The gun, with its silencer, slid across the tiled floor. The man was handcuffed and lifted up by the arms behind his back. How he got the gun through security no one knew.

It was over in a minute and Italia was dead. Her jet-black hair was splayed over the table, but this time combined with dark red blood.

As he was led out of the courtroom, Zucchini Sam laughed and exclaimed one more "Bada Bing!"

No one knew who the man was except Detective Lippa. He recognized him from his mug shot taken many years ago. Samuel Mancuso. The man they had been looking for just this morning. Like the rest of the courtroom gallery, Lippa was shocked to his core with what had just transpired. He gripped the seat in front of him and shook his head in frustration and sadness as he looked upon the deceased victim. He now had another case on his hands.

This case was now closed.

About the Author

Elly Stevens was born and raised in Rochester, New York, in a family of story-tellers. "Remember when…" were often the first words at every family gathering. At a very early age, Elly was writing fictional stories and scripts with characters from the 1950s TV shows like *The Thin Man* for her and her friends to act out. In her teens at Nazareth Academy, she worked on the staff of the high school's literary magazine, *Spectrum.*

Following her dream of writing, she joined the Publications group at Eastman Kodak Company where she held several positions including technical editor and the consumer-relationship management (CRM) team project manager for KODAK Digital Camera e-mail marketing campaigns.

After Elly retired in 2004, she enjoyed her rural house and gardens on Lake Ontario, and, with her husband Jeff, had the house torn down to the studs and rebuilt. She also tended to her granddaughter, primarily in her pre-school years, and reveled in a "second childhood."

It wasn't until a former co-worker, **Joe Janowicz,** contacted Elly to edit his first novel, *Bang-Bang You're Dead,* in 2018 that she picked up writing again. Her first book, a memoir, *Searching for Serenity in My Crazy Life,* allows a peek into many of the real-life experiences with her family and friends. Her second book, *Dangerous Passion,* is a fictional story of fallible relationships, choices, passions, and ultimately… murder.

www.AuthorEllyStevens.com

Ken Wheaton, Cover Artist

Dangerous Passion cover artist **Ken Wheaton** has worked on comics for Bongo, IDW, Image, Moonstone, and Airwave. Most notably, he's contributed artwork to various *Simpsons* comics and books, as well as drawing several issues of *Popeye*. His other comic book work includes the *Back to the Future, Official Adaptation of Mr. Magoo's Christmas Carol,* and issues of *I Dream of Jeannie, The Phantom, El Mucho Grande-Wrestler for Hire, Kolchak: The Night Stalker, Jetta,* and *Buckaroo Banzai-The Prequel.* He also drew a special commemorative premium comic celebrating the 80th birthday of cartoon icon *Popeye.* He was a contributing artist to the hardcover books *C. Montgomery Burns' Handbook Of World Domination* and *Bart Simpson's Manual Of Mischief.*

As a freelance illustrator, Ken has worked on local and national projects, contributing artwork and designs for a series of television ads for clients Toyota, McDonald's, and Wegmans.

He recently served as editor of *Munster Memories: A Coffin Table Book* with **Butch Patrick**. Ken is currently working on a new comic project, *Dreamer,* with creator **Joe Janowicz.**

Ken teaches several popular comic book production workshops each summer, which yield anthologies of student work and prepares tweens and teens interested in entering the field. He has also worked with The Strong National Museum of Play in Rochester, New York, as a teaching artist.

More of Ken's work can be seen at
www.kenwheaton.com

SEARCHING FOR SERENITY
in My Crazy Life

The real-life stories of a baby boomer
In Rochester, New York.

Everyone has a story to tell; **Elly Stevens** has a "lifetime" of stories to tell. Journey down memory lane as Elly shares 70 years of life with her family and friends. Travel with her through every significant stage of her life from early childhood memories, growing up in an ethnic neighborhood, her first kiss, her marriage, the birth of her son, the trials and tribulations of motherhood while balancing a challenging career at Kodak, learning how to face and embrace retirement, the delight of a granddaughter, the passing of friends and family members, and the beginning of new "life" at age 70.

Searching for Serenity in My Crazy Life. Fun, fascinating, and memory provoking. Growing up doesn't mean growing old. Growing up is a life story.

Available on Amazon and Barnes and Noble online.
www.AuthorEllyStevens.com

The Naked Dead

By Joe Janowicz

When the clothes come off, the killing begins.

Someone is killing naked people. Paradise Lost, an international naturist resort is holding a major "bare all" nudist and adult swingers convention. When a celebrity guest is found floating "bottoms up" in one of the luxury outdoor pools, the local police are called to investigate. Another naked guest is found dead in the window display of an on-premise concessions shop. Both victims have bite marks in their necks and are drained of all their blood. Is this the work of a "real life" vampire, or a crazed psychopath pretending to be a vampire?

Detective Jamie Parker and Police Officer Jim McKenna are given the undercover assignment to stay on site as a couple and search for any clues. To blend in, they have to go "au natural" and mingle with the guests.

More mysterious deaths continue as the killer plays a game of cat and mouse with Jamie, intending to make her a victim. Never having been to a nudist resort, let alone walk around in public wearing only sunglasses and a smile, Jamie discovers that you don't need clothes to catch a killer.

Amazon online and selected bookstores